"I need you to do me a very *special* favor."

Max smiled mysteriously as he spoke.

Angela grimaced. "Do I have the right to refuse?"

"Of course," he said with a casual shrug. "I'm not planning to force you. But you must understand..." he paused for effect "...that if you refuse, I shall consider our agreement broken. And that can have only one consequence—you'll be forced to say farewell to your business." As he uttered the sweetly threatening words, the smile never left his lips.

Angela shivered inwardly. "You leave me with a lot of choice," she shot back hostilely. "And what exactly is this favor?"

"I want you to come away for the weekend with me. But not as my secretary—as my lover."

Stephanie Howard is a British author whose two ambitions since childhood were to see the world and to write. Her first venture into the world was a four-year stay in Italy, learning the language and supporting herself by writing short stories. Then her sensible side brought her back to London to study Social Administrations at the London School of Economics. She has held various editorial posts at magazines such as *Reader's Digest, Vanity Fair,* and *Women's Own,* as well as writing free-lance for *Cosmopolitan, Good Housekeeping* and *The Observer.*

LOVE'S VENDETTA
Stephanie Howard

Harlequin Books

TORONTO • NEW YORK • LONDON
AMSTERDAM • PARIS • SYDNEY • HAMBURG
STOCKHOLM • ATHENS • TOKYO • MILAN
MADRID • WARSAW • BUDAPEST • AUCKLAND

ISBN 0-373-17171-4

LOVE'S VENDETTA

Copyright © 1992 by Stephanie Howard.

CHAPTER ONE

'ARE you looking for anything in particular, Miss Smith, or were you merely acquainting yourself with the contents of my office?'

At the sound of a man's voice coming from the doorway, Angela spun round abruptly from the display cabinet to face him.

And that was when she got a very big shock indeed, for he was not at all what she'd been expecting.

She smiled at him brightly, disguising her surprise. 'Ah, Mr Fielding... I didn't hear you arrive.'

Angela had assumed he would be considerably older, red-faced and overweight from an excess of good living. But the man who stood so eloquently before her in the doorway carried not a spare ounce on his six-feet-plus frame. Beneath the dark blue suit every inch was hard-packed muscle. And the head of sleek dark hair and the chiselled suntanned features proclaimed him to be, at the most, in his middle-thirties.

Nevertheless, she had no doubts that he was the man she had come to see. Physically, he might not be as she had imagined Max Fielding, but there was an air of arrogance and self-assurance about him that left her in no doubt as to his identity.

He was the man whom she detested with every fibre of her being. The man who had financially ruined her father and left her mother a penniless widow.

He smiled now, and let his gaze drift with open interest over her, taking in the thigh-high skirt she was wearing, the shiny, clingy sweater, the perilously high heels—an outfit that revealed every curve of her slender body and that she had chosen deliberately and with infinite care.

It was a million miles away from her normal way of dressing, but it was an essential part of her carefully worked-out strategy. Quite simply, for want of a better word, it was bait.

And he was biting, Angela thought with a small prickle of satisfaction as, without haste, his eyes dark with lazy sensuality, he allowed his attention to drift back to her face.

'If I may say so, Miss Smith, it is perfectly obvious that you were unaware of my arrival. Had you heard me,' he continued, his tone lightly cutting, 'I doubt very much that I would have caught you hovering with such interest around my display cabinets.'

'I wasn't hovering, Mr Fielding. I was simply admiring the contents.'

Angela's tone was polite as she rebutted his accusation, suppressing the urge to match his subtle hostility. She must not antagonise him. Her mission was too important. She simply *had* to get the job as his temporary personal secretary. Everything depended on that.

She widened her smile. 'I was admiring your collection.' As she said it, seductively, she fluttered mascaraed eyelashes. 'You have some truly exceptional pieces in those cabinets. Not the sort of collection one would expect to find in an office.'

'Is that so?' He had not moved from the doorway, and there was something about the way he stood there, his tall, powerful physique seeming to dominate the space around him, that made Angela feel, illogically, as though she were his prisoner. A fly caught in a corner of his web.

'And what would one expect to find in an office? Tell me, since you appear to be an expert on the subject.' As he smiled, condescendingly, Angela sensed with sudden certainty that it was no accident that she had suddenly felt like a captive. That was precisely how he wanted her to feel.

She stepped away from the corner cabinet and into the centre of the room, deliberately dispelling that illusion.

And, inwardly, she smiled. If only he knew! *He* was the fly and *she* was the spider!

She shrugged her slim shoulders and tossed back her chestnut hair, currently arranged in a mane of bimboesque curls. 'Oh, I don't know,' she answered. 'I suppose I'd expect to find books on business technique—or, in your case, on banking and investment . . .'

As she paused she was aware of the dark eyes on her, drifting from the line of her high, taut breasts to the elegant curves of her long, long legs. I've got him! she thought triumphantly. Behind all that hostility, he's definitely interested in what he sees. She had judged his taste in women perfectly!

With another flutter of her lashes, she added, 'It's a little unusual to come across such a collection of beautiful objects in an office.'

'You like my collection?' His tone was lightly contemptuous. He didn't give a fig whether she liked it or not.

'I think it's exquisite. Particularly these two.' She swivelled round and pointed with her finger to an African wood carving and a magnificent jewel-encrusted egg. 'That is Fabergé, isn't it?' she enquired with wide, impressed eyes. 'Obviously, you're quite a connoisseur.'

'So I'm told.' Her flattery simply amused him. As he smiled he held her eyes for a moment. 'I've been told I'm a connoisseur in many different areas.'

She knew what he was getting at and she had heard that story, too, that he was a hungry connoisseur of glamorous, sexy women. That was why she'd come here, decked out like a Christmas tree, in an effort to take advantage of his one known weakness and persuade him to take her on as his temporary assistant.

His smile lingered. 'And are you a connoisseur, Miss Smith?'

She suppressed a blush at the subtle *double entendre*. The sort of women he liked did not blush easily.

She smiled back at him boldly. 'I wouldn't say that, but I do have a taste for beautiful things.'

'Then we have something in common. I, too, appreciate beauty.' He paused a beat and held her gaze as he added, 'And whenever I see something I find beautiful, I'm afraid I simply have to have it.'

As he said it he smiled sensuously, his eyes caressing her openly, and Angela was aware of a sudden flare of panic as she guessed at the thoughts that were going though his head.

She had better be careful. This man was far from being the clumsy, crude operator she had expected, and whom she had known she would have no difficulty in handling. Max Fielding was a different bag of tricks altogether. Max Fielding was smooth. Max Fielding was dangerous.

He looked at her now with those piercing dark grey eyes that each time he looked at her sent a shiver through her. 'So, now you know why I have art objects instead of books in my office. I like to surround myself with beautiful things.'

His gaze roamed over her face with its brightly lip-glossed mouth, wide sea-green eyes, heavily accentuated, and he smiled again. 'I find beauty inspires me. Especially beauty that shines, that dares to flaunt itself.'

Then, as she flinched and fought to hide it, he added, his wide mouth curling, 'And, as a collector, as I've told you, I don't just admire it, I like to possess it. I have a compulsion to take it and make it mine.'

Angela was suddenly wishing that she'd worn sackcloth and ashes. Or alternatively that she could take to her heels and run. Yet she had to stand firm.

She swallowed drily. 'Well, I just love your collection,' she murmured with a cracked smile.

He continued, 'Besides, I don't need to fill my wall space with books on banking and investment. I'm already sufficiently well-acquainted with my profession.'

Such endearing modesty! His appeal grew by the minute! Yet Angela was grateful for the sudden switch in subject.

'Oh, I know you are. I'm aware of your reputation.' And as she cast a quick smile at him, hating him, despising him, and noting once again how her flattery slid off him, it struck her that beneath that boundless outward arrogance there undoubtedly lurked a core of hard steel. This man was not just hard and unbending on the surface, he was hard and unbending all the way through.

And powerful with it. She could sense a strength of character that simultaneously impressed and scared her.

All the more of a challenge, she decided as she put to him in a tone of earnest mock-sincerity, 'And, of course, to work for a man of your reputation would be both a privilege and a pleasure . . .'

He smiled a knowing smile and stepped out of the doorway, cutting her short with a wave of his hand. 'Kindly take a seat, Miss Smith,' he commanded, 'and let's get on with what we're both here for.'

He had waved her in the direction of the huge mahogany desk that stood with its back in the curve of a wide bay window. As Angela seated herself in one of the button-backed chairs arranged in a semicircle round the front of the desk she caught a glimpse of the magnificent view beyond the window. The green stretching lawn, the mass of flowerbeds, the elms and sycamores in their bright autumn finery.

Again she experienced that first jolt of surprise that had unsettled her slightly on her arrival. For she had not expected to find the notorious Max Fielding in such an exquisitely beautiful setting, nor in an office like this, on the ground floor of his sumptuous mansion, filled with exotic *objets* and antique furniture. A man with a heart as hard as his did not belong in such surroundings.

Oblivious of her judgement, he proceeded to settle himself in the green leather swivel chair on the other side of the desk. And, as he turned for a moment to glance at the monitor in one corner, Angela caught a glimpse of aquiline profile—curved nose, high cheekbones and a well-defined mouth that would know how to inflict both pain and pleasure. The latter for his amusement, the former as a matter of course.

Then he turned to face her. 'As you know, I'm the head of Solid Gold Investments. It's me you'll be working for—if you get the job.'

The last five words were spoken as a challenge. You're a long way from having landed the job yet! he was warning her.

Angela nodded politely. 'I hope I do, Mr Fielding.' And quite involuntarily her stomach tightened. She *had* to get the job. It was absolutely crucial.

He leaned back in his chair, his demeanour suddenly businesslike. 'So, Miss Smith, perhaps you'd like to tell me why you think I should take you on as a temporary replacement for my personal secretary?'

Angela's response had been carefully prepared. She smiled a keen smile. 'Certainly, Mr Fielding.' Then she crossed her knees carefully, adjusting her tiny, narrow skirt before launching into a formidable account of her considerable experience and impeccable skills.

In conclusion, she assured him, 'I think you'll find that all these claims are fully backed up by the personal report provided by the agency.' This she knew to be a fact. She had prepared the agency report herself.

Max Fielding nodded. 'Yes, I've read the report. I have to say I found it most satisfactory...'

As he said it he raised one straight dark eyebrow and, simultaneously, Angela's expectations.

His gaze lingered on her face. A sadistic smile touched his lips. 'Most satisfactory in *some* respects... But considerably less than satisfactory in others.'

'Oh?' Angela suppressed a flutter of alarm. Just bear in mind, she quickly reminded herself, that what this man says is not necessarily what he means, and that one of his chief pleasures is tormenting others.

She smiled a composed smile. 'In what respects less than satisfactory? I'd be grateful if you'd tell me which particular points you're not happy with. I'm sure I can offer some explanation.'

'I'm sure you can.' Max Fielding smiled across at her—again that cynical alligator smile. 'But whether your explanation would be to my satisfaction is another matter entirely, of course.'

'At least give me the chance.' Angela smiled co-operatively. 'I might surprise you,' she challenged, her smile pinned to her face.

'Who knows? You might. Though I tend to doubt it.' Max Fielding smiled a diminishing smile. Then abruptly he leaned back in his swivel chair and surprised her by observing, 'Tell me one thing . . . I get the impression that you want this job badly.' He narrowed his dark eyes at her. 'Why is that?'

Angela felt a nervous flutter inside her. The answer was easy. The job would, she hoped, provide an opportunity to achieve justice. To win back on behalf of her widowed mother the money Max Fielding had stolen from her father.

But he must not know that. He must know nothing about her. She must convince him that this was a straightforward job application.

She regarded him earnestly. 'I need the money. When you do temporary work, as I do, a gap can be disastrous. Like everyone else, I have bills to pay. And temporary jobs are a little thin on the ground here in Cambridge at the moment. This is the only one going over the next couple of weeks.'

If she had hoped he might be moved by her supposed dilemma, such hopes were about to be rudely dashed. Not a shadow of sympathy softened the harsh features as he watched her impassively over the desk.

'Why do you do temporary work?' he put to her in a direct tone. 'Why don't you find yourself a permanent job? With your qualifications that shouldn't be hard.'

'Oh, I intend to. Later,' Angela assured him. 'But just for the moment temporary work suits me better.'

'I see.' His dark brows grew together as, thoughtfully, his grey eyes scanned her face. 'May I ask when the last temporary appointment you held was?'

It was the question Angela had been praying he would not ask her. Evasively she answered, 'The agency report lists all my appointments——'

'But without specifying dates. That is what I'm not happy about. Perhaps now, as you promised, you would be good enough to provide some answers.'

It would have been so easy just to lie in the report she'd written, to have put in a few harmless details that weren't quite true. But her scrupulously honest nature wouldn't allow that deception, even though she had known it might make her task easier.

So she had restricted herself to omitting tell-tale dates, in the hope that he would confine himself to checking her credentials and not notice that the dates were missing. But Max Fielding, as she was fast learning, noticed everything.

'Well?' He was watching her, waiting for her answer.

'I'm afraid it was a little while ago,' Angela answered evasively, praying she wouldn't blush and betray her sense of guilt. 'Quite a little while ago, in fact,' she conceded.

'And by quite a little while ago do you mean weeks or months?' Relentlessly, he continued to press her.

'Months, I'm afraid.' About thirty-six, to be truthful! 'But in the meantime,' she hurried on before he could demand that she be specific, 'I've been keeping up all my secretarial skills...'

'Working for whom?'

'For myself, as a matter of fact.' In that, at least, she was being totally truthful.

'And why aren't you still working for yourself?'

Angela shrugged, her heart beating furiously inside her. How to fend him off without perjuring herself totally? The very last thing he must be allowed to find out was that she *was* still working for herself, running the very employment agency that had supposedly sent her for this interview!

She took refuge in evasion. 'You know how things are... You must have seen the statistics... Most small businesses collapse within their first year...' She gave a resigned shrug. 'One does one's best, but one mustn't be too surprised if one's efforts don't come off.'

'I supposed one mustn't.' His tone was strangely scathing. She could not quite make out the expression in his eyes. Suddenly nervous, she held her breath as he was about to go on—but, to her relief, one of the phones on his desk began to ring.

'Excuse me one moment.' He reached for the receiver and half swivelled round in his chair as he spoke into it.

Angela breathed a silent sigh of thanks that, for the moment, she had been allowed to escape from that tight corner. Under pressure, she feared, she might have given herself away.

She glanced across at his profile as he spoke into the phone. He was astute, as she had known he would be, and she was vulnerable, because deceit and deception did not come naturally to her. But her cause was just, she reminded herself sharply. Her ends more than justified the means she must employ. And she must not blow this golden opportunity.

Her eyes drifted down to the sliver of mini-skirt, exposing long shapely legs ending in saucy high-heeled shoes. The disguise—which she had had to splash out on; she had nothing like it in her wardrobe!—was more than just bait, she secretly acknowledged. It also allowed her to keep a comfortable distance between her real self and what she was doing. As the real Angela, she might have felt uneasy, but dressed like this it was a great deal easier. She was playing a part. This wasn't Angela.

There was a click from across the desk as the receiver was replaced. Angela raised her eyes, but he had not turned to look at her. He appeared to be gazing out through the wide bay window.

'So, Miss Smith, the story so far is that you have recently failed in a private business venture and have decided for the moment to work as a temporary secretary...'

As he paused a sudden shaft of autumn light poured through the window to illuminate his profile. The lines of his face, Angela thought to herself, were about as soft and compassionate as those of a can-opener. Every feature seemed imbued with the same harsh power that glinted from the unexpectedly long-lashed grey eyes. The dark, glossy hair reflected light like a steel helmet.

He turned slowly to look at her, making her heart jump strangely. 'At least, that is the story you would have me believe?'

Angela swallowed. 'Why shouldn't you believe it?' She tried to smile. 'Why would I lie to you?'

'Why indeed?' He swivelled his chair to face her and leaned back a little so that his features were in shadow. 'Personally, I can think of several reasons.'

As his eyes bored into her Angela's insides turned to water. Did he know who she was? Had all her efforts been wasted?

With difficulty she kept her eyes fixed on his face. 'What reasons, for example? I can't imagine.'

'Can't you? Then let me make a few suggestions. Perhaps you are a thief, simply using the ruse of working for me in order to gain entry to my home. My home, even more than my office, is filled with many objects whose sale would ensure that you would never need to work again.'

'But that's ridiculous!' Relief surged through her. Thank heavens, he was on the wrong track entirely! 'I'm not a thief. Of that I can assure you.'

'And would you admit it if you were?'

'Probably not.' Angela looked him in the eye. 'But you can take my word for it, I have no intention whatsoever of robbing you.'

'Why should I take your word? You have not been honest with me. I can tell, Miss Smith, that you are hiding something.' As she flushed a little he narrowed his eyes at her. 'And you have already betrayed an interest in my valuables. Were you not busy checking them out when I came into the room?'

'I was simply admiring them——'

'No doubt you were.' He leaned suddenly across the desk towards her. 'People who hide things, I find, tend to have something on their consciences. I wonder, Miss Smith, what guilty secret is on yours?'

'I have no guilty secret.' Angela was genuinely alarmed now. She looked across at him urgently. 'I'm not a thief, Mr Fielding. Please believe me. I haven't come to steal from you.'

He rose slowly from his chair. He was shaking his head. 'Why should I believe you? This building is full of treasures. And the personal history you have presented to me is, to say the very least, sketchy.'

She could feel all her hopes and plans trickling through her fingers. She had blown her chance to bring him to justice—and it was her mother who would pay for it with a life of near-penury.

It was that thought that spurred her into action. As he came round the desk Angela jumped up to face him. 'I'm an excellent secretary and I need this job badly. I have a mother who depends on me. Please don't turn me down.'

He was standing less than an arm's length away, so close that it felt as though he was almost touching her. She could sense against her skin the virile warmth of him and smell in her nostrils his cool, clean scent.

His eyes bored into her, eyes that she could see now were touched with flecks of gold around the irises. 'You say you have a mother who depends on you ... Is that an invention or is it the truth?'

'It's the truth. I swear it.' As a matter of fact, it was.

'And she will suffer if you fail to get this job?'

Angela nodded. 'Yes.' That was a lie.

'I see.' He seemed to lean back on his heels to look at her. Then he smiled, showing a flash of very white teeth. 'In that case, I cannot be hard-hearted ...'

Angela dared to smile a half-smile as he thrust his hands into his pockets.

'Since the arrangement is only for a couple of weeks, I shall go against my instincts and take you on trust.'

'Thank you, Mr Fielding.' Relief rushed through her—though she was far from convinced by this display of humanity. She sensed that, in spite of his deliberate attempt to scare her, he had intended to hire her all along. In the hope of adding her to his collection.

She recalled his earlier words: 'Whenever I see something I find beautiful, I'm afraid I simply have to have it.' She remembered, too, the look in his eyes as he'd said it and the memory caused her heart to flutter.

One thing was for sure, she had no easy task ahead of her. Somehow, using all her female weaponry, she must distract his attention from what she was really up to, yet at the same time she must keep him at a safe distance. And in Max Fielding's case, that was a very long way away.

But now was not the time to start worrying about these problems. She should be feeling pleased. She had crossed the first hurdle.

Resolutely, she pushed her anxiety from her and smiled into Max Fielding's handsome, hateful face. 'I really am most dreadfully grateful.'

'Save your gratitude.' His smile had hardened. 'Over the next couple of weeks you will learn, Miss Smith, exactly what it means to earn one's salary.' Without moving, he seemed to take a step towards her. 'And I shall also be keeping a very close eye on you.'

Angela wanted to step away. His nearness oppressed her. But she forced herself to stand her ground without flinching.

'Take my word for it,' he repeated. 'A very close eye.'

Without a flicker Angela met the steel-hard gaze. Not half as close an eye as I'll be keeping on you! she silently answered.

CHAPTER TWO

'CONGRATULATIONS! I knew you'd do it!' Jill raised her wine glass and winked across at Angela. 'So, now you've been admitted to the devil's inner sanctum, all you have to do is find some evidence against him.'

Angela pulled a face. 'I hope I'm up to it. All this Mata Hari stuff isn't really my style.' She ran her fingers through her glossy chestnut hair, brushed free now of its lacquer and bimboesque curls. 'I'm sure he's going to suss what I'm up to.'

'Of course he isn't. He doesn't know who you are. For once, be grateful for a name like Smith. There are so many of them around that he'll never connect you with your father! Anyway,' Jill added, smiling, 'he seems to think it's his art treasures you're after, so it's those he'll be keeping an eye on, not the files that really interest you. That is, when he's not chasing you round the office!' she added, teasing.

'Don't remind me!' Angela laughed, and grimaced as she sat back against the cushions of Jill's sofa, drawing her black-trousered legs up beneath her and pushing back the sleeves of her cable-knit sweater. 'The man's a maniac, a real skirt-chaser. You should have seen the way he kept looking at me with those come-to-bed eyes!'

She sighed. 'But the disguise was an inspiration. He obviously likes his women big, bold and brassy. I probably wouldn't have got the job if I'd gone to the interview looking like my real self.'

Her real self was the way she was looking now, her beauty—though Angela would never have described herself as beautiful—subtly enhanced by the barest minimum of make-up and the stylishly classic clothes she liked to wear.

She smiled across at Jill, her partner, friend and confidante. 'It's all thanks to you that I've even got this far. If you hadn't been an old friend of Fielding's secretary I would never have been handed such a golden opportunity.'

Characteristically modest, Jill smiled and shrugged. 'That was pure chance, my bumping into her like that. We hadn't set eyes on one another for years.'

'Pure chance, perhaps, but absolutely crucial,' Angela acknowledged gratefully as she took another sip of her wine.

If Jill hadn't had that chance meeting with Sally, Fielding's secretary, and told her all about Ace Personnel, the employment agency she was now running—fortunately without mentioning her partner by name—Sally would never have contacted her to hire a temporary replacement for herself when she was unexpectedly called away on urgent family business. And Angela would never have had the chance to apply for the position.

Angela raised her glass to her. 'Between you and my cousin Denis, I reckon I have the best two

friends in the world. At a time when I really needed
good friends...' She broke off as her throat seemed
to fill with painful tears at the memory of her
father's recent death. Then she took a deep breath
and finished what she'd been saying. 'You're wonderful friends, both of you. Worth your weight in
gold.'

Jill leaned towards her and softly touched her
arm. 'You've been through a lot lately, Angela,'
she said kindly. 'But you're coming through it all
with flying colours—and you'll win in the end.' She
smiled. 'I know you.'

Such faith, Angela thought, touched, as she
drove home later that evening. I just hope that faith
proves to be justified. Max Fielding in the flesh had
proved to be even more alarming an adversary than
she had envisaged him. It was going to take all her
determination to best him.

She drew up outside the rented apartment block,
on the outskirts of the historic city of Cambridge,
and paused for a moment to gaze up at the dar-
kened windows of the apartment that these days
she called home. Sadness poured through her. It
was all so different from the little mews cottage that
had once been hers. But that was lost now. Thanks
to Fielding.

She climbed out of the car and slammed the door
shut. Every misfortune in her life, it sometimes
seemed, was somehow related to the despicable Max
Fielding. Certainly her father's disastrous financial
state, revealed on his death just a matter of a few

months ago, had been brought about by Max Fielding's dishonest dealings.

All her father had left his widow, Angela's distraught and grieving mother, had been a mountain of debts that had left Angela no choice but to sell up her cottage in order to pay them and at the same time keep a roof over her mother's head. If it hadn't been for the generosity of her cousin, Denis, who had invited her to share his apartment rent-free, accommodation-wise she would have been in a serious fix.

Rents were high—when one could find a place to rent—and she was still in the process of paying off her father's debts. Jill had offered her a bed in the tiny flat she shared with Eddie, but to have taken her up on that kindness would have been an imposition. The strictly temporary arrangement with Denis was different. Her cousin was hardly ever at home, and for weeks on end Angela had the apartment to herself.

She hurried across the pavement towards the front door. It was Denis, too, who had told her about Fielding.

'He's a crook,' he'd advised her when she'd confided her discovery, made while going through her father's private papers, that he'd had financial dealings with Fielding's Solid Gold Investments. Denis had pointed to an article in one of the business papers linking Max Fielding with a prominent City stockbroker, currently on trial for cheating his clients and leading them into financial ruin.

'My guess is that what's happened to your father's money is that Fielding has it safely stashed away in one of his Swiss bank accounts.'

The more Angela had thought about it the more she had agreed with him, and the more determined she had become to expose Max Fielding.

She took a deep breath now as she pushed open the front door. She had two weeks in which to do it, starting from tomorrow. For her mother's sake, she mustn't blow it.

'Allow me to show you round the office, Miss Smith, then both of us can get down to some work.'

Angela smiled up at him, parting brightly lip-glossed lips. 'Ready when you are, Mr Fielding. Personally, I can't wait to get started.'

'Good.' He paused and let his eyes drift over her, not for the first time since she'd walked into the office. 'May I say you're looking quite stunning this morning? That bright, vibrant red really suits you.'

'I'm glad you think so.' Angela fluttered her lashes as the dark eyes continued to drink her in. Look all you want to, she was thinking, but try to touch and you're a dead man!

And again it struck her that Cousin Denis had been right. Fielding really did have a penchant for glamorous women. But then, he was not exactly drab himself. To judge by the sharp cut of the mid-grey suit he was wearing, the quality of the claret silk tie at his throat and the suppleness of the alli-

gator shoes on his feet, he was a man who cared
about the way he looked.

And there was no denying that he looked good.
He would have no trouble at all attracting in droves
those glamorous women he was so partial to. With
those arrogant dark looks of his and that air of
sensuality, all he would need to do was snap his
fingers. In fact, she decided, if I didn't know so
much about him I might find him rather attractive
myself.

That acknowledgement, which flitted into her
mind unsummoned, shocked her slightly. She felt
vaguely unsettled. Instantly, she chased it away.
Such a thought was both foolish and irrelevant. Not
in a million years could she be attracted to such a
villain.

'Perhaps we should begin our little tour by my
stating what must already be obvious.' As he spoke
he leaned against a corner of the desk and looked
into her face with a lightly sardonic smile. 'As you
will have gathered, the rooms which comprise my
office also happen to be the ground floor of my
home.'

Angela nodded. 'Yes, I was aware of that.' Then
she frowned. 'Don't you have an office in London?
That surprises me in your line of business.'

'Don't be surprised,' he quickly assured her. 'I
also have a base in London. But I find that with a
bit of careful organisation I can conduct the bulk
of my business from here.'

He smiled. 'I bought this house a couple of years
ago with the intention of using it as a weekend re-

treat. I'd had my eye on the place since I was a student here, years ago. But I soon discovered that I liked living here so much that I decided to move my office here as well.'

Angela regarded him with curiosity and censure. So, he was a Cambridge graduate. She might have guessed. He had that poised, cultured air of so many of his fellows. What a pity he was such a scoundrel. Such a waste of a privileged education.

She looked back at him. 'I don't blame you for wanting to live and work here. It's a lovely part of the world.'

'Have you always lived here?'

'Most of my life. My parents moved here when I was five years old.' She had been about to add, 'when my father was appointed manager of one of the stores in the city centre'. But, luckily, she managed to stop herself in time. She must be more careful, she reminded herself sharply. The less Max Fielding knew about her, the better.

He straightened a little. 'So, as I was saying, the rest of the building houses my private quarters.' He nodded. 'That door over there in the corner marks the boundary between office and home. For that reason, Miss Smith, I must insist that you consider that door to be out of bounds.'

Angela glanced at the door, then raised her eyes to his. Thanks for the warning, she was thinking. But out loud she assured him, 'Of course, Mr Fielding. Naturally, I respect your privacy.'

'Good.' His iron-grey eyes surveyed her, almost as though he was looking for something. 'Nor-

mally I keep the door locked to minimise the risk
of accidental straying. But even I, at times, can be
forgetful. In such circumstances, I trust, you would
not take advantage?'

So he still thought she was after his worldly pos-
sessions. Angela smiled to herself. Little did he
know!

She fluttered her lashes. 'Of course not, Mr
Fielding. I wouldn't dream of such a thing.'

'Unless, of course, I invite you personally.' He
held her eyes. 'That would be different entirely.'

I'll bet! Angela grimaced inwardly and said
nothing. Don't worry, she was thinking, I'll never
pass through that door. *Especially* if you invite me
personally!

He held her eyes a moment, then turned away
abruptly. 'Follow me!' he commanded as he headed
on long strides towards the oak-panelled door at
one side of his desk. 'This is my secretary's office,'
he informed her, pushing the door open. 'And yours
for the duration of your stay here.'

It was a delightful room, a smaller version of his
own, the desk positioned by a window that over-
looked the gardens.

'How lovely!' Angela looked round with interest.
'Perhaps you could just quickly show me where
things are. It would save me having to go searching
among your secretary's things.'

'Quite so.' As he said it he caught her eye. 'More
to the point, among *my* things, Miss Smith. All my
files and papers are kept in this room, apart from

those pertaining to what I'm currently working on...'

He waved an elegant hand at the units that lined the walls. 'In there you will find...alas, no Fabergé eggs...' he allowed himself a flicker of a smile '...just a great deal of vital information.' He had stepped towards the nearest set of units, pulling open the panelled mahogany doors to reveal drawers containing paper files and piles of computer disks.

'In this cupboard, for example, you will find details of all my clients.' He closed the doors and opened another cupboard. 'In this, details of the UK companies I deal with. Overseas companies are in that one over there.'

With Angela right at his elbow he went through each cupboard in turn, ending with the cupboard nearest her desk. 'The master files are kept in here. If you can't track something down these will tell you where to look for it.' He pushed shut the door and turned to look at her. 'Is there anything you want to ask me?'

As a matter of fact, there was. Angela stepped forward and pointed. 'That cupboard in the corner... You forgot to tell me what's kept in there.'

A pair of shuttered grey eyes looked back at her. 'No, I did not forget,' he answered in a crisp tone.

'I'm sorry, Mr Fielding, but I'm not mistaken. You definitely forgot to mention that cupboard.'

He shook his head. 'I repeat, I did not.'

'But——'

'Miss Smith——' he held up his hand to silence her '—I did not forget to mention that cupboard. On the contrary, I quite intentionally omitted it.' A cool smile curled around his well-shaped lips. 'And I omitted it for a very good reason. That cupboard contains information to which only I have access. And for that very reason it always remains locked.

'So you see, Miss Smith...' his eyes flashed her a warning '...that cupboard and its contents comprise the one corner of this office which really does not concern you in the slightest.'

'I see.'

'I hope you do.'

Angela nodded. 'Absolutely.'

And, feigning a lack of interest she was far from feeling, she turned her back towards the cupboard in question as he glanced at the gold watch on his wrist and observed, 'And now, if you don't mind, I think both of us have work to do.' He indicated a pile of disks and files on her desk. 'There are some files there that require updating. I suggest you make that your first task this morning. When you've finished with that, come and see me. No doubt I shall have found plenty more for you to do.'

Angela slid behind the desk, feigning eagerness, leaned forward and switched on the computer.

'If you have any problems, just give me a shout.'

'Yes, Mr Fielding.'

'But I trust there won't be any. I have rather a lot to get through this morning.'

As he turned on his heel and headed towards the door Angela watched him go with a secret smile on her lips. Inside, her heart was beating with excitement, an excitement she could scarcely contain.

Once the door had closed behind him, she rose from her seat and crossed to the cupboard in the far corner. She reached out to test the handle. It was locked, as he had warned her.

She took a step back and stared at it fixedly, as though by sheer force of will-power she might be able to open it. For suddenly she knew that behind that locked door lay the secrets she had come here to uncover.

Somehow, in spite of Max Fielding's threatening presence, she had to find a way inside it. And she had only two short weeks in which to do so.

A week later Angela was deeply worried. She had still not found a way to gain access to the crucial files.

Not that she wasn't constantly on the alert to every opportunity that came her way. A dozen times at least in the course of a day Max Fielding would appear suddenly in her office and either remove something or replace something from the corner cupboard. And each time he left the room again Angela would hurry to check if he had accidentally forgotten to relock it.

After all, he himself had said, 'Even I, at times, can be forgetful.' But so far, alas, his memory had not failed him.

He was less meticulous, however, about keeping his desk locked. On more than one occasion he had left his office briefly without bothering to lock his desk and remove the key. Angela had seen the key dangling tantalisingly from the lock. And she happened to know that it was in the bottom right-hand drawer that he kept the key to the secret cupboard.

'It would be so easy to take the key, unlock the cupboard and sneak the key back again without him knowing,' she had confided in frustration to Jill. 'But I can't risk doing that. He could come back at any moment to remove something or put something back in the cupboard, and he'd notice instantly that it was unlocked—and who else could have unlocked it but me?'

She'd sighed a helpless sigh. 'What I need is for him to go off somewhere for a couple of hours, then I could copy as many of the files and disks in the cupboard as possible and take them home and study them at my leisure.'

And then, out of the blue, came the opportunity she had prayed for.

It was on Tuesday evening that Fielding suddenly announced, 'Tomorrow we have to go up to London. I have an important meeting in the City and naturally I'll need you along to take notes.'

Angela's heart sank. A whole day out of the office. That only left her Thursday and Friday. Suddenly things were starting to look desperate.

And then a flash of inspiration came to her rescue. 'What about Mr Burton?' she reminded him. 'He said he'd drop by about eleven tomorrow morning to pick up that file he needs so urgently.'

'Couldn't you mail it?'

'He said we weren't to mail it. He was very emphatic about that.'

Max Fielding frowned and considered for a moment. Then he sighed. 'I guess, in that case, I'll have to leave you here. Can you manage the office for a whole day on your own?'

It was an effort to stop herself from cheering. Angela nodded. 'Of course I can, Mr Fielding. I can get on with that backlog of correspondence.'

That night Angela found it hard to sleep. She lay staring into the darkness and endlessly rehearsed how she would take the key from Fielding's desk and open up the secret cupboard, then spend the afternoon copying the disks and files.

That would be the easy part. The hard part would be deciphering the information that she found there. But, thankfully, Denis, who knew a little about financial matters, had promised her his services in that direction. Between them, she felt certain, they would eventually uncover the dishonest dealings that had ruined her father—and kept Max Fielding in smart suits and alligator shoes, not to mention the Rolls-Royce, as big as a troop ship, that she'd seen parked ostentatiously outside the office.

He was already at his desk when she arrived at the office next morning, gathering up the files he would need for his London meeting.

He glanced up to greet her. 'You're looking cheerful. You must be looking forward to spending the day on your own.'

'Not at all.' Was her excitement that obvious? 'It's just that it's such a lovely day.' She glanced a little nervously towards the window, grateful to see that the sun really was shining. In her state of excitement she had barely noticed.

He nodded to one of the chairs ranged opposite his desk. 'Take a seat,' he told her, 'while I just run through a couple of things I'd like you to do today.'

Suddenly as nervous as a cat, Angela did as she was bid, only half listening as he proceeded to reel off the list of jobs that he had prepared. And all the while her eyes were fixed on his desk and the key that dangled like a half-promise from the lock.

'That's it, then.' Fielding picked up the papers on his desk, pulled open the top drawer and dropped them inside. 'I reckon that should keep you out of mischief.'

As he said it, he smiled, a mocking little smile, and, to her horror, his hand began to reach for the key.

If he locked the desk she was totally lost. Angela felt panic rise up in her throat. Suddenly she knew she had to do something.

She sat forward abruptly. 'Mr Fielding...' her brain was scrabbling for some ruse to distract him '...Mr Fielding, can you give me a number where I can reach you? It probably won't be necessary, but just in case.'

He gave her a narrow look. 'I've just told you it's in the file.' As he spoke his hand continued to hover over the key. Angela's heart stopped as he seemed about to turn it. Then he paused unexpectedly and instead reached for a pencil and with a small shrug scribbled a number on his notepad. He pushed it towards her. 'Here's the number, just in case you can't find it in the file.'

Angela's heart seemed frozen in her chest. She took the piece of paper and rose to her feet. 'Thank you,' she smiled. Her eyes were on him, though she hardly dared watch what he was about to do next. And every atom of her strength at that moment was focused on willing him to forget to lock up the desk.

'I think that's everything.' The dark grey eyes looked back at her. 'I'll go now and leave you to get on with things.' He held her gaze for a long, unsettling moment, and suddenly the tension inside her was unbearable. Her nerves were drawn so tight that she felt they must snap.

He rose to his feet and pushed back his chair. 'I'm not sure when I'll be back,' he told her. There was another endless pause as he reached for his briefcase. 'But if I'm not back before it's time for you to leave, lock up for me. You know the procedure.'

Angela nodded. 'Certainly, Mr Fielding.' She could scarcely speak for fear and excitement. For at last he was stepping away from the desk and heading on swift strides for the door.

It was in the same instant as her prayers were answered that Angela realised overwhelmingly the magnitude of what she was planning. And knew, too, with stunning certainty, that if he was to find out he would destroy her utterly and take pleasure in doing so.

For at least twenty minutes after he had left the office Angela sat motionless at her desk, simply staring at the corner cupboard. Never, even remotely, had she done something like this before, and suddenly she wasn't sure if she had the stomach to go through with it.

She shook her head miserably and frowned at the desk. Had she gone to so much trouble only to back out now? Was she really such a coward?

She forced herself to think of her poor widowed mother, existing on a pittance when she should be living in comfort. Max Fielding had done that. He was to blame.

It was enough to galvanise her into action. She rose to her feet and on resolute steps strode through the doorway that led to Fielding's office. Without breaking her stride she crossed to his desk and with trembling fingers pulled open the bottom right drawer. The key to the cupboard was in its usual place—in a little silver box in one corner.

She lifted it out. It felt cool and heavy. With an excited, nervous shiver she clutched it in her hand. Then, moving like an automaton, she turned on her heel and headed back into her own office.

Quickly she crossed to the corner cabinet and stuck the key in the lock, held her breath and slowly turned it.

There was no sudden cataclysm. No thunderbolt from heaven. All that happened was that the door swung open, soundlessly, to reveal its secrets.

After that, her brain seemed to switch to automatic. Working as fast as she could, she took the paper files and began putting them sheet by sheet through the Xerox. Then, once she'd finished those, she started on the disks, copying them on to the blanks that she'd hidden in her desk.

It was so easy. So simple. The operation was going like clockwork. She glanced at her watch. It was still only lunchtime. By the time Max Fielding got back to the office, supposing he actually got back before she left, the cupboard would be locked, the key back in its place, the vital evidence stowed safely in her car and every sign of what she'd been up to carefully erased.

But, even as she congratulated herself on her triumph, there came a sudden sound from beyond the open door. As she whirled round belatedly, the colour drained from her face. Max Fielding was standing in the doorway, watching her.

He smiled at her strangely, surveying the scene. 'My, my, this looks interesting,' he observed.

CHAPTER THREE

In that moment Angela died a thousand deaths. She was incapable of moving, glued to her chair. She stared back at Max Fielding in stunned, helpless silence. She had been caught red-handed. There was nothing she could say.

He stepped into the room and closed the door behind him, then stood for a moment, his eyes boring into her, his hands thrust deep into the pockets of his trousers.

'Please don't waste my time by offering excuses. You see, I know exactly what you were up to.'

Angela swallowed. Her mouth was as dry as cardboard. 'You came back early,' was all she could think of to say.

'Indeed I did.' He smiled a cold smile. 'Although "came back" is not strictly accurate. You see, I've never been away. For the past few hours I've been at home upstairs, enjoying some lunch and a glass or two of wine.'

Angela blinked at him, astounded. 'Y-you what?' she stuttered. 'You mean you didn't go to London?'

'No, I'm afraid I didn't. There was no meeting. I confess I told you a little white lie.'

'But I don't understand.' Her brain was swimming. All at once she had the uneasy suspicion that she had fallen into some carefully laid trap.

Fielding seemed to read her mind. 'Yes, you fell for it quite beautifully. It couldn't have worked out better if we'd rehearsed it.'

'You mean——?' Angela waved helplessly at the open corner cupboard and the files and disks that were strewn about her desk. 'You mean you knew I was planning to do this? You mean you knew it all the time?'

'I'm afraid I did. So sorry to disappoint you when you were thinking that the whole thing was your own clever little idea. I even knew precisely how you'd do it, and when. I picked today because it was conveniently quiet for me.' He smiled a smile that made her shudder. 'You see, I've been preparing for this moment since the day you came to work for me.'

Angela sat back in her seat, dumbfounded. 'But why? It doesn't make any sense. Why would you encourage me to spy on you?'

Max Fielding took a seat on one of the chairs next to her desk. There was anger in his face, dark and thunderous, but at the same time he wore an air of total unruffleability, and more frightening than his anger was this total self-control. Had he ranted and raged she would have felt less threatened. This icy self-possession made her blood run cold.

Without haste, he unbuttoned his immaculate grey jacket and sat back easily in his seat. 'Oh, don't misunderstand me. I have no wish to be spied on.

At least, not by an accomplished spy. For, I think
you will agree, your efforts in that direction have
proved to be somewhat less than accomplished. In
fact, sadly for your sake, they've been a total
failure.'

He waved a hand towards the Xeroxes and copied
disks. 'Naturally, I intend to confiscate all of this.
Your efforts, you see, have been a total waste.'

'But why would you even want me to go through
the motions?' Angela, in turn, glanced at her wasted
endeavours. 'What was the point of letting me get
as far as this?'

Max Fielding simply smiled. 'Perhaps,' he put to
her, 'it suited my purposes to gain a slight edge of
bargaining power.'

'Bargaining power?' Angela was totally baffled.

'Yes, Miss Smith, bargaining power. I think
you'll agree that this unfortunate incident has sub-
stantially altered the balance of power between us.
And, sadly again for your sake, to my advantage.
You have, as the expression goes, been caught, Miss
Smith, with both hands in the cookie jar.'

Angela regarded him with growing discomfort.
He was right, she was compromised, totally vulnerable. She felt her blood run cold within her. He
had her at his mercy.

But she put on a brave face. 'I don't know what
you're talking about. You may like to think you
have, but you don't have any hold over me.'

'You think not, Miss Smith?' He leaned back in
his chair and crossed his long legs at the ankles.
'You could be right, of course.' He seemed to con-

sider. 'But it seems to me the situation is rather different. For one thing, if we fail to strike a satisfactory bargain...'

'Bargain?' As he paused, Angela frowned across at him, not liking in the slightest the implications of what he was saying. 'I can't see me entering into any bargains with you.'

'Can't you?' He shook his head at her. 'Perhaps this will change your mind...' Then, in a tone of voice so reasonable that it was chilling, he elaborated, 'If we fail to strike a satisfactory bargain I fear it is within my power to put an end to your career.'

Angela blinked like someone walking off an unexpected step. She felt her stomach jolt sickly within her.

Then she pulled herself together. Surely he was bluffing? All he was doing was trying to scare her, taking for his own perverse amusement all the sadistic enjoyment he could from this hideous situation.

She tilted her chin at him. 'You're talking nonsense, Mr Fielding. I have no career for you to put an end to. You're forgetting I'm just a temporary secretary.'

'Ah, yes, I was forgetting...' He smiled a cobra smile. 'The young lady who so sadly failed in her efforts to run her own business has no career that I could possibly damage...' Then, like a cobra, he pounced, going straight for the jugular. 'On the other hand, I suspect that the real Miss Smith has a great deal more to lose.'

Angela's stomach clenched like a fist inside her. Her fear seemed to swamp her, making her feel faint. With difficulty she managed to look back at Fielding. 'You're talking in riddles,' she accused in a light tone. 'I'm afraid I haven't a clue what you mean.'

Suddenly, in desperation, it was she who was bluffing.

'Haven't you, Miss Smith?' Max Fielding's gaze was candid. 'Forgive me if I call you a liar. You see, I know that you know exactly what I mean.'

'Really, I don't.' Inwardly, she was weeping. She felt as though she were being roasted on a spit.

He turned the spit a half-turn, savouring her agony as he did so. 'Let me put it to you like this ... then perhaps my meaning will become more clear to you.' He sat back a little in his chair and narrowed his grey executioner's eyes at her. 'Consider the possibility that I reveal to the local community that the respected co-owner of Ace Personnel has been masquerading as a temporary secretary in order to gain access to my private files— and has been caught red-handed breaking into them ...'

As she blanched he continued, 'I tend to suspect that I would really have very little trouble stirring up sufficient controversy to ensure that the agency was closed down within the week.'

Angela could scarcely bear to listen. What she was hearing were all her blackest nightmares come true. 'You mean you know who I am?' she demanded faintly. 'Is that something else that you've known all along?'

'I'm afraid it is.' He smiled a smug smile. 'You see, you're not quite as clever as you thought you were. And I, sadly for you, am a whole lot cleverer.'

Damn his cleverness! Angela did not answer. Suddenly she understood the whole scenario. He had set her up from start to finish, planting in her mind the fiction of his forgetfulness when in reality he had a mind that was as sharp as a razor. His desk, she realised now, he had left open deliberately.

She eyed him resentfully as he added, 'Oh, by the way, that file of Mr Burton's that concerned you so greatly... I took it round personally to his house yesterday evening. I thought it better that we shouldn't be disturbed today. That might have proved a little embarrassing.'

Angela scowled at him. She had forgotten about Mr Burton, and the risk of embarrassment was the least of her worries! And suddenly she felt angry at having been taken for such an idiot. She had fallen for all his lies hook, line and sinker.

'I suppose this sort of fakery comes easily to you,' she accused him. 'Cheating and lying and deceiving people is, after all, something you do every day.'

Max Fielding did not bother to answer the accusation. Defence was not his way. Attack was more his style.

He said, 'Your cousin Denis will be disappointed. He was rather banking, I suspect, on the success of your mission.'

As it had clearly been intended to, that observation left her speechless. Not only did he know she was a partner in the agency, it appeared he knew everything about her. If he knew about her cousin, he would know also about her father.

He was watching her, savouring the look of horror on her features. 'Poor old Denis. You've let him down badly.'

That baffled her slightly. Angela narrowed her eyes at him. 'Let Denis down how?' she queried. 'What are you talking about?'

He shook his head slowly. 'You know what I'm talking about. Denis is going to be extremely disappointed.'

That only made her feel even more baffled. What were all those strange allusions to Denis?

She frowned across at Fielding. 'I haven't a clue what you're talking about.' She felt suddenly uneasy, confused and oddly threatened. 'What's going on? What are you up to? What game are you playing and why did you plan all this?'

Max Fielding betrayed a flash of impatience. He rose to his feet and stepped abruptly towards her to stand, tall and threatening, at the edge of the desk. 'Please don't play the innocent with me, Miss Smith. As I told you at the start, I know what you're up to—you and your clever little cousin, Denis.'

He paused. 'What *I'm* up to is simply this...' Angrily he swept the disks and Xeroxes from her desk, sending them to the floor in a plastic and paper avalanche. 'My little game, as you call it, is simply explained. Its aim is to put a stop to you and your dear cousin!'

The explicit violence of the gesture was shocking. Angela watched him in stunned silence for a moment as he strode through the debris, crushing files underfoot, then proceeded to pace the room backwards and forwards, as though he could scarcely contain his rage.

But his insistence on hauling Denis into things was totally puzzling. Angela waited till he seemed to have calmed down a little, then in a quiet voice she assured him, 'Denis had nothing to do with any of this. The whole thing was entirely my idea.'

For a moment he said nothing, just stood and looked at her, his face a stiff, hard mask of fury. He turned away abruptly. 'OK, then, have it your way. Let's pretend you don't know what I'm talking about. In the end it'll make no difference to the outcome. That is something I can promise you!'

There was a ruthless resolve in his voice that chilled her. It was the tone of a man who would stop at nothing.

Angela watched him warily from beneath lowered lashes and knew that it would not be wise to reveal her fear. 'You still haven't answered my question,' she insisted boldly. 'What exactly do you plan on doing with me, and what is this whole preposterous business about?'

A small scornful gleam came into his eyes. 'You really do play your part extremely convincingly. Anyone but myself would believe in your innocence.' His expression sobered. 'What all this has to do with, since you profess to have no idea, is a small outstanding question concerning your father.'

At the glib, insensitive reference to her father Angela felt her whole body stiffen. How dared he have the gall even to mention her father? After the way he had destroyed him, did he have no shame?

She clenched her fists and rose slowly to her feet. 'I'm surprised you have the nerve to raise the subject of my father, considering what you did to him.'

Black eyebrows soared. 'Considering what *I* did to him?' He paused and raked her face with dark and scornful eyes. 'Is this the line that Denis advised you to take in the unfortunate event that you were found out?'

How quickly he had dropped the subject of her father! Perhaps, after all, he had a shred of conscience.

Angela glared at him. 'Are you deaf or something? I keep telling you, Denis has nothing to do with this.'

'So you do. I keep forgetting.' His eyes seemed to burn right through her, like lasers. 'Is what you're actually trying to tell me that Denis is nothing more than your lover?'

That winded her totally. Angela felt her jaw drop open. 'What did you say?' she demanded disbelievingly.

He simply smiled. 'Come, come, Miss Smith. You don't have to pretend. I'm pretty broad-minded.'

Angela took a step towards him. He had finally gone too far. 'I'm really not interested in the breadth of your mind. But I can assure you, none the less, that Denis is not my lover.'

'Of course, of course.' He leaned against the cupboard at his back, folded his arms across his chest and looked unblinkingly across at her. 'I understand he's away at the moment. You must be feeling a little lonely.'

'I'm not lonely in the least. I like living alone.'

'Do you? In that case, why did you move in with him?'

Angela took another angry step forward. 'If you don't mind my saying so, I really don't think that my living arrangements are any concern of yours. And they are most certainly not anything I intend to discuss with you. If you have anything to say to me about all of this——' she gestured vaguely at the chaos at her feet '—that's a different matter entirely. I admit I did wrong and I apologise. But, since no harm's been done, couldn't we just forget it?'

Max Fielding laughed. 'I suppose we could...'

But, as he looked at her, Angela knew better than to hope. All she could see was warm malice in his eyes.

He did not disappoint her as he continued, very slowly shaking his dark head, 'But I'm afraid that just to forget it is not my intention.'

'Do you intend to go to the police?' Her stomach tightened as she said it. His threat that he could ruin her had not been an idle one.

He was still leaning against the cupboard, long legs crossed casually at the ankles. 'That is not my intention either—for the moment.' He smiled a cruel smile and continued to watch her. 'What I do next really rather depends on you.'

Suddenly Angela was remembering that earlier reference to a bargain. She felt an uneasy flicker inside her. If he demanded money she had none to give him. In fact, she had nothing to give him at all.

He straightened suddenly and took a step towards her. 'I can see you're wondering what nature of bargain I'm intending.' He took another step nearer. 'And whether you'll be able to deliver.'

Angela wanted to step away. He was standing much too close now. But she gritted her teeth and remained where she was. She would not let him see how much he distressed her. That, she sensed, would only give him pleasure.

He stopped just a matter of inches away and let his gaze rove over her, insolently appraising, as though he was stripping the clothes from her flesh.

'Now that we finally know who we are...' he dared to reach out and run his fingers unhurriedly along the collar of the glitzy blouse she was wearing—yet another of her special purchases '...now that all has finally been revealed, I'm looking forward to getting to know you better.'

Angela flinched visibly. What was he suggesting? Surely the bargain he had in mind did not involve the crude bartering of her body?

He smiled strangely as she tried to back away abruptly and caught hold of the thin, shiny cloth with his fingers. 'I suspect that behind all those bright feathers you enjoy wearing lies the soul of a deeply sensuous young woman. As I said, I shall greatly enjoy finding out.'

'You'll never find out!' Angela pulled away sharply. 'You can threaten what you like. I'd sooner lose my business!'

'Is that a fact?' He had still not let go of her. With the smallest of efforts he jerked her towards him. 'I wonder what Jill would have to say about that? Remember, my dear Miss Smith, it's her business, too.'

Angela felt sick. Momentarily, she had forgotten that. Suddenly she was overcome by a wave of black misery. In her bid for revenge all she appeared to have done was jeopardise her professional future and that of her friend.

And she had no right to sacrifice Jill. Jill had nothing to do with any of this.

She felt like weeping. She closed her eyes tightly. 'Tell me what you want,' she said, 'and I'll do it.'

It seemed she had no choice but to make a deal with the devil, though somehow, she vowed, she'd find a way to wriggle out of it.

'That's more like it.' Max Fielding stepped away from her, finally releasing his grip on her blouse.

Angela dared to look up at him. 'So, what do you want? Don't beat about the bush. Come straight out with it.' In spite of her inner anguish, her tone was scathing. Without the need to put them into words she had expressed her views on men like him who were prepared to stoop to blackmail to gain sexual favours.

Max Fielding's expression didn't alter, though she sensed he had understood her message perfectly. 'Sit down,' he told her. 'Make yourself comfortable and listen very carefully to what I have to say to you.'

Angela seated herself numbly in the chair behind the desk and watched with distaste as he took the seat beside her. He leaned towards her, 'What I have in mind is this. Since you're not a bad secretary, and since you're so pleasing to have around—I warned you that I love to be surrounded by beautiful objects—I've decided to keep you on for a little while longer. For the time being you shall continue to work for me.'

Relief and despair went rushing through her. 'I can't stay on here! I've a business to run! And what about your own secretary?' she pleaded. 'She'll be coming back soon and she'll want her job back.'

'Wrong, Miss Smith. She won't be coming back. You see, I've given her extended paid leave. So please don't worry about depriving her of her job.'

As he knew very well, that was not her principal worry. Angela straightened in her chair. 'It's ridiculous,' she protested. 'Why keep me on when you already have a secretary and you know that I'm needed at Ace Personnel?'

He leaned back in his chair. 'Don't worry about my motives. My motives, Miss Smith, are no concern of yours. Let's just say that, for the

moment, I prefer to keep you on as my secretary—
and that you, as I see it, have no choice but to
agree.'

That was something Angela could not argue with.
As pointless as his demand appeared to be, she
would refuse to co-operate at her peril.

She took a deep breath and regarded him
squarely. 'And is that it? Is that the extent of your
demands—that I stay on here for a while as your
secretary?'

'For the moment that is all.' He smiled mysteriously. 'As to the future, let's just play this by ear.
I may or may not decide to make further demands
of you.'

Angela glared across at him. So she was still not
safe. But for the moment, she sensed, it would be
wise not to argue.

'For how long do you foresee this arrangement
continuing?' Her voice was croaky as she asked the
question.

'For as long as it suits me.' He raised dark eyebrows, then suddenly he smiled, an alligator smile.
'Please don't look so distressed, Miss Smith. Who
knows? You may come to enjoy our arrangement.'

Angela rather doubted that. She looked back at
him and shuddered. 'Don't count on it, Mr
Fielding,' she advised him. 'I rather suspect I'll
loathe every minute.'

He smiled a knowing smile. 'We'll see,' he said
mysteriously. Then he rose to his feet and, turning
towards the door, gestured at the chaos of litter on
the floor. 'Destroy the disks and shred the Xeroxes,

and please don't even think of trying to pull anything. There are hidden cameras in each corner of
this room—just one small point I forgot to
mention.'

Angela resisted the temptation to glance up and
check his words. He wasn't lying, she could see that
in his face. And again she cursed herself for
handling this so badly. What a rash, impetuous fool
she had been.

He had turned away and was heading back to his
office. But then, abruptly, he paused and turned to
her. 'Oh, by the way, you can drop the ridiculous
disguise now. It doesn't suit you, and, contrary to
what someone has told you, I don't go for women
who look like the front line of the chorus.'

He smiled a slow smile. 'That's another reason
for keeping you on, to find out what you look like
when you're not dressed up in all that junk.' His
smile broadened. 'I suspect you're not only deeply
sensuous, but stylish and classy. Just my type.'

As he turned away again Angela glared at him,
hating him. He had trounced her on all counts, even
seen through her disguise, but he was wrong if he
thought he could exploit the hold he had on her.
No matter what threat he dangled over her, she
would never succumb to his sexual advances.

Never, she vowed grimly. I'd sooner burn in hell!

CHAPTER FOUR

THE first thing Angela did when Fielding released her that evening was go round to Jill's flat and re-count the sad story.

'I can't tell you how sorry I am,' she told her friend guiltily. 'Do you think you can manage for a while longer on your own?'

Jill was sympathetic. 'What a bastard that Fielding is. Of course I can manage. Don't worry about it, Angela. But perhaps you ought to forget about doing any more spying. I don't think it would be a good idea to take any more chances. He sounds like a dangerous man to me.'

Angela nodded in agreement, but made no promises. The only thing that would make her time with Fielding bearable was the knowledge that she could turn it to her advantage by continuing to work secretly against him. Besides, it would be a betrayal of her parents not to.

But, all the same, she could appreciate Jill's fears. 'Don't worry,' she assured her, 'I'm going to play things very safely. I owe it to you, apart from anything, to get out of this mess as quickly as possible.'

After a quiet little dinner with Jill and her boyfriend Eddie, Angela was feeling a little better. She went back to the flat, suddenly exhausted, looking forward to a good night's sleep. But as soon as she opened the door the phone began to ring.

She picked it up, praying it wasn't Fielding. No doubt, since he knew so much about her, he also knew her home phone number. But to her relief, of all people, it was Denis.

'Hi, Angela, I've been trying to get hold of you all evening.' He paused an instant. 'Are you all right?'

'Of course I'm all right, I was round at Jill and Eddie's.' She sat down on the sofa. 'How are you?'

'I'm fine. I'm just phoning to tell you I'm not going to be back for another three weeks.' Another short pause. 'Have you had any luck with Fielding? Have you managed to dig up any dirt about him yet?'

'No, I'm afraid not. But don't worry,' Angela assured him. 'I'm going to be staying on with him for a little while longer, so there's still time to dig up what I'm after.'

'OK. Good luck. Listen, I have to go now. But remember to get in touch with me just as soon as you get hold of anything.'

'Don't worry, I won't forget. Thanks for phoning. Look after yourself. I'll see you when I see you.'

As she laid down the phone Angela leaned back against the cushions. Why, she was wondering, hadn't she told Denis the whole story? Why hadn't she recounted the disaster that had happened and the weird, unspecified accusations that Fielding had made against her cousin? Surely Denis had a right to know?

She sighed to herself. The whole thing's too confusing, and far too complicated to discuss over the phone. That's the only reason I didn't tell him. I'll tell him all about it when I see him.

It was a genuine excuse. She *was* genuinely baffled, Angela decided later as she got ready for bed.

One thing that baffled her was that claim of Fielding's that not only did he know what she was up to, but he had also known all along, from the very beginning. For the more she thought about it, the more she felt certain that he hadn't.

Perhaps what had planted the doubt in her mind had been partly that unexpected brief reference to her father. Surely he would have said more, offered her lies and excuses, if he'd known that what she was doing was because of her father? And what had also caused her to doubt was the way he had so misguidedly insisted on trying to tie Denis into the affair.

In a way it seemed too good to be true, but she had a growing suspicion that, in reality, Max Fielding was unaware of what she'd been looking for. He believed she'd been after something else.

Not so surprising, she rationalised cynically as she climbed beneath the bedclothes and turned out the light. He no doubt had many dark secrets hidden away.

She stared into the darkness. So, she still had that advantage—that he did not know what she was really after. She smiled to herself. She must hold on to it. She was going to need every advantage going.

'That's more like it! I was right when I suspected that underneath those gaudy feathers you were a classy and most attractive young woman.'

Next morning Angela walked into the office dressed in an outfit from her legitimate wardrobe—a slim camel skirt and a blue silk blouse—her hair soft and unlacquered, and on her face only a fraction of the amount of make-up she'd been wearing recently.

It was a relief to be able to be her old self again, but the last thing she needed was Max Fielding's approval.

She threw him a cool look. 'How very clever of you. No doubt you're an expert when it comes to judging women?'

'I have only one complaint.' He ignored her cutting query. 'Red suits you better than that blue you're wearing. I told you that already. I like you in red.'

'It's a colour I rarely wear,' she lied, glaring at him furiously.

'Then change your habits. Wear it more often. To please me. Surely that's not much to ask?' As she continued to glare at him he smiled amusedly. 'After all, in the beginning you were keen enough to please me. You went just a little over the top, of course, but at least the desire, quite clearly, was there. Why this sudden change of heart?'

'There's been no change of heart. It was never my desire to please you.' Such outspokenness might not be wise, but she could not resist it. 'All I ever wanted was for you to give me the job.'

'And who was it who told you that you'd get it if you dressed yourself up like the front line of the chorus? Was it Cousin Denis, by any chance?'

'It might have been. And he was quite right, wasn't he?' She narrowed her eyes at him. 'You did give me the job.'

'Indeed I did.' He smiled arrogantly across at her. 'But only because I was shrewd enough to see what you were really like under that preposterous disguise.' He paused. 'And you really are a most desirable young woman. Although, as I said, you look better in red.'

In that case, I shall never again wear red to the office!

That was the promise that went through her head. Yet she knew she was being silly, that such an attitude was counter-productive. She should be grateful, should she not, that she could please him so easily, without having to deck herself out, as he had put it, like a chorus girl? After all, until she had completed her mission, she needed this uncomfortable liaison to endure.

She pulled herself together and smiled compliantly. 'In future I'll try to bear your preferences in mind.'

'Good girl.' His tone was gratingly condescending. 'Not that I'm really complaining, mind you. As I said, you're looking very attractive this morning.'

'Thank you.' Angela couldn't quite suppress a grimace. 'And now, if you've finished awarding points for my appearance, perhaps you wouldn't mind if I got on with some work?'

'Go right ahead. That's what you're here for.' To Angela's irritation, his response was to smile at her. Her attempt at sarcasm had simply amused him. 'There's a pile of work waiting for you on your desk. Let me know when you get through it.'

Then, as she turned sharply away from him and headed for her office, he added, 'Oh, by the way, I'll be requiring you to work late this evening.' He paused a beat before offering insincerely, 'I do hope that's not going to inconvenience you?'

'Not in the slightest.' She would not give him the satisfaction of knowing that, in fact, she had made plans to visit a girlfriend. But as she stepped through the doorway into her office she was seething. It looked as though her penance had well and truly begun!

That assessment of the situation proved pretty accurate. In the days that followed late nights and skipped lunches literally became a way of life. But at least that was all she had had to contend with. Fielding had made no demands on her other than those strictly secretarial.

But then, halfway through the following week, he announced, 'Tomorrow we'll be going up to

London. I have a couple of meetings in the afternoon.'

Angela nodded, her expression businesslike. 'Very well.' Then, as he continued to watch her, she added, 'Is there more?'

'As a matter of fact, there is. We'll be having dinner together afterwards, so I suggest you bring along something dressy for the evening. You can change in the office. That's what I'll be doing.'

Angela wasn't at all sure she liked the sound of that. 'Is this a business dinner? Will there be clients there?'

'No, Miss Smith. Just you and me.' He smiled amusedly. 'Won't that be cosy?'

'I wish I could agree.' Angela looked back at him with annoyance, not appreciating his sense of humour in the slightest. 'If you don't mind, I think I'd sooner take a rain check. Since it's not business, I'd prefer to spend the evening at home.'

Max Fielding shook his head. 'I'm afraid that's not an option. You'll be having dinner with me whether you like it or not.'

Angela's heart sank. She knew it was pointless arguing, but she couldn't just meekly accept this intrusion.

'Why do you want to inflict such an unwilling companion on yourself? I'm sure,' she added with a bite of sarcasm, 'you have plenty of ladyfriends who would jump at the chance.'

Max smiled. 'I suspect you're probably right, but I'm afraid the offer is not negotiable. The others, alas, will just have to wait their turn. Tomorrow evening I've decided to bestow the honour of sharing my dinner table on you, Miss Smith.'

Some honour, Angela thought, as with barely fettered anger she rummaged through her wardrobe later that evening, searching for something suitable to take with her.

Her fingers hovered over the bright red silk sheath dress that had cost her a fortune and which she simply adored. She hated to wear it to a dinner with Max Fielding, but it really was the obvious choice. As she kept telling herself, it was in her interests to please him.

It was with equal bad humour that less than twenty-four hours later, in the luxurious ladies' room at Fielding's London office, she pulled on the red sheath and fixed the belt at her waist, then glowered at her reflection in the mirror.

Perhaps she ought to have tarted up the dress's simple elegance with a gaudy brooch or an over-the-top necklace? Or else fancied up her hair and piled on the lip-gloss? For she was suddenly aware that for the first time in her life she was finding it uncomfortable just being herself. Without her gaudy feathers, as Fielding had called them, she felt oddly exposed, oddly vulnerable.

Vulnerable? Surely not? She blinked at her reflection. Surely the only reason she was feeling uncomfortable was because she detested the fact that Fielding appeared quite genuinely to appreciate the type of girl she really was? Who wanted to be appreciated by a monster?

When she stepped out of the ladies' room Fielding was waiting in the hallway, leaning against a marble pillar, arms folded across his chest.

His reaction could not have been better geared to annoy her. He looked her up and down and gave a low whistle. 'Stunning,' he approved. 'I really like it.'

Then he stepped towards her, offering her his arm as he did so. 'Let's go. I don't know about you, but I'm starving.'

Studiously, Angela ignored the proffered arm. She might have agreed under duress to accompany him to dinner, but he was mistaken if he thought she had any intention of playing the role of blushing escort!

It was as though he had read her mind. He smiled as he pulled the door open, and suggested, it seemed to Angela, deliberately to annoy her, 'In the light of the circumstances, I think it would be appropriate for us to drop the formalities for the evening.' He held her eyes. 'Feel free to call me Max, and I'll feel free to call you Angela.'

Ignoring her scowl, he led her out to the Rolls. 'The restaurant's not far. We'll be there in five minutes. I hope you like French,' he added with a smile as he unlocked the passenger-door and held it open for her.

Angela mimicked a smile back at him. 'I'd prefer a McDonald's. Something fast, so we can get this charade over quickly.'

She felt him smile as she climbed inside. 'That's not the attitude, my dear Angela. Food, like sex, is something that should be savoured. One needs two hours minimum to enjoy either to the full.'

As he slammed the door shut Angela glared out of the windscreen. Her stomach had lurched strangely at that remark about sex. And no wonder, she decided. It had been tasteless in the extreme.

The restaurant, in the heart of Mayfair, was as chic and expensive-looking as she had expected it would be. And it was clear that Max was a regular customer as they were shown, amid a flurry of obsequious smiles, to a prestigiously placed table in one candle-lit corner.

'What will you have to drink?' As the waiter handed them their menus he smiled across at her. 'How about champagne? Let's make this an occasion to remember.'

'Like the sinking of the *Titanic*?' Angela scowled across at him. He was wrong if he thought she could be wooed by his false charm.

To her annoyance he just looked back at her with amused, unbothered eyes. 'So, champagne it is.' He gave their order to the waiter. Then he smiled across at Angela. 'What an endearing sense of humour.'

'Not as endearing as yours,' she shot back at him. 'I suppose you think it's highly amusing, subjecting me like this to the ordeal of your company?'

In reply, he simply smiled infuriatingly across at her. 'There are many who would give their eye-teeth to endure such an ordeal. So, stop scowling, dear Angela, and try to enjoy this rare privilege.'

Vain beast! Angela gave her attention to the menu, dismissing him with a sharp toss of her head.

But even as she sat there, studiously ignoring him, she had to confess that there was truth in what he said. On the surface, at least, he was a most desirable escort.

He was wearing the same grey suit he'd been wearing earlier, but he'd changed his shirt for a plain crisp white one, a perfect foil for his sleek dark good looks, and for the brightly stylish red silk tie—which she'd earlier observed with a flicker of irritation matched almost perfectly the red of her dress.

Anyone looking at them would think they had planned it. Anyone looking at them would think they were a couple.

How wrong could you be? She slid him a glance beneath her lashes and was mildly horrified at the way her stomach tightened. She had never denied that he was attractive, but, all the same, knowing what she did about him, it was a trifle gross of her to entertain these physical reactions. The only physical reaction she should be entertaining was revulsion.

'Have you decided yet?'

As he asked the question Angela glanced up unhurriedly to meet his eyes. This time, reassuringly, her stomach did not tighten. Instead, she noticed how relaxed he was looking, possibly more relaxed than she had ever seen him. The observation served only to irritate her further.

Pointedly she ignored his question. Instead, she frowned at him. 'Perhaps you'd like to tell me . . . is there any particular reason for this dinner? Is there some aspect of my work that you wish to discuss with me?'

He leaned back in his chair. 'Maybe there is and maybe there isn't. Perhaps this little dinner is purely for our pleasure.' As he spoke he bestowed on her an infuriating smile. How much he enjoyed his sense of power over her. The fact that she hated him for it merely added to his enjoyment.

In proof of this assessment, he added, smiling, 'It is always a pleasure to have dinner with a pretty woman.' His eyes were on her. His smile grew broader. 'And, by the way, it was really sweet of you to wear red for me.'

That annoyed her, and added to her discomfort. 'I'm not wearing it for you,' Angela shot back instantly, hating the way the denial sounded so defensive. 'It just happened to be the only suitable thing in my wardrobe.'

Max winked knowingly. 'No need to be coy. As I told you, I appreciate the gesture. There's just one thing I'm wondering . . .'

He paused for a moment, as the waiter reappeared with two fizzing champagne flutes. Then, as the waiter moved away again, he continued, 'Did you wear red for me, I mean *really* for me—as a woman making a gesture to please a man? Or was it a rather more cynical decision, meant to appease rather than please me?'

Full marks for vanity! And for self-delusion! That it should even enter that arrogant head of his that she had any motivation to please him as a man!

Angela narrowed her sea-green eyes at him. 'Are you one of those men who think that everything a woman does is inevitably aimed at pleasing some man? The way she dresses? The way she comports herself? All for the benefit of some male audience?'

'Why, isn't it?' He was incorrigible! He even smiled as he said it, rejecting in advance her scornful rebuttal.

'Most certainly it isn't!' Angela sat back, exasperated. 'Women dress and do things for all sorts of reasons—not the least being quite simply to please themselves!'

'But also to please men.' He was insistent. 'Surely you wouldn't be so dishonest as to deny that?'

'Perhaps. Occasionally. If the man merits it.'

He smiled. 'So, you did not wear that dress to please me?'

'I wore it because it was all I had that was suitable.' Angela clenched her jaw at him. 'I already told you that.'

'So you did.' He was watching her, smiling. 'Forgive a somewhat hackneyed Shakespearian quotation, but "The lady doth protest too much, methinks".

'But don't worry,' he added before she could answer that. 'I find your reticence rather appealing. Contrary to what I led you to believe initially, I have no taste for collecting what is there for the picking. What really excites me are those elusive treasures that can only be tracked down with skill and persistence.'

It was like a sexual challenge thrown at her across the table. Angela was glad the waiter chose that moment to reappear, pen poised, ready to take their orders.

Yet she was annoyed, too, that he was capable of throwing her so easily. She was quite capable of faking total immunity to his games-playing, but deep inside he disturbed her and confused her.

As the waiter moved away again, Max leaned back in his seat. 'But enough about me. Let's talk about you.'

Angela took a mouthful of her champagne. 'But you already know all about me,' she countered.

'Not all.' Idly, he fingered the silver cutlery. 'Tell me about you and Denis, for example. How long has this partnership of yours been going?' As he said it his tone altered subtly. There was a sudden hint of darkness at the backs of his eyes.

Angela threw him a narrow look. 'What partnership are you talking about? Denis and I happen to be cousins.'

'Distant cousins, in terms of blood ties. Isn't that the case?' Max queried in response.

'I suppose so. He's the son of my father's cousin. But I've always thought of him as being a proper cousin. After all,' she added, 'as you probably know, since you seem to know so much about me, he lived with us for a while after his parents were killed. That was when I really got to know him.'

She'd been twelve at the time, Denis sixteen, and, though he'd only stayed with her family for just over a year, Angela had grown to think of him almost as a brother.

She flicked Max Fielding a critical look. 'Your little theory that we're lovers is quite preposterous. There has never been—could never be—anything like that between us.'

Max held her gaze. 'Then why did you move in with him? It seems rather an unlikely thing for a girl who owns her own home to do. Unlikely, unless, of course, she's romantically involved.'

So he did not, after all, know everything about her. She informed him cynically, 'You're just a little out of date. I no longer own my cottage.'

Black eyebrows lifted. 'Wasn't that rather rash of you? Where will you live if the romance with Denis falls through?'

At that moment the waiter arrived with their starters—snails in garlic for Angela, battered whiting for Max. Angela breathed deeply until the waiter had departed. 'I sold my cottage because my mother needed the money in order to pay off my father's debts.'

She hadn't meant to say it, but suddenly she couldn't resist it. 'As you may know,' she added, every syllable an accusation, 'my father died leaving nothing but debts.'

His eyes narrowed as he watched her. He said nothing for a moment. Then he spoke. 'Yes, I was aware of that sad fact. It must have been quite a blow for your mother.'

His poise was so unshakeable that it was almost scandalous. How could he sit there and mouth such platitudes when it was he who'd been responsible for her parents' financial tragedy?

But with an effort of will Angela held back that accusation. For the moment she would keep what she knew to herself.

'So you sold your cottage and moved in with Denis...' He was still watching her. He had not touched his food. 'And whose idea was that—yours or his?' he queried.

'His, since you're so interested.' Angela watched him with disapproval, remembering how the invitation had come the same evening that she had confided to her cousin her plan to go after Fielding. She picked up her cutlery. 'But it's just a temporary measure, till I get my finances together and find a place of my own.'

'I see.' He shook his napkin over his lap. And the eyes that a moment ago had been watching her so closely glowed once more with that amused, mocking light that never failed to infuriate Angela. 'So I can take your word for it that you and Denis aren't lovers?' He took a mouthful of his wine and surveyed her with sudden interest. 'Is there anyone else I ought to know about?'

'*Ought*?' Angela raised a caustic eyebrow. 'Mr Fielding, there's nothing you *ought* to know about me! Our agreement, as I recall, gave you no such rights.'

'Max. Please don't be formal.' Then he smiled. 'Let me rephrase that... Do you have a boyfriend? Is there someone special in your life?'

'There may be and there may not be.' It was none of his damned business! 'And what about you, Mr Fielding?' she put to him, ignoring his entreaty to use his Christian name and deliberately trading insolence for insolence. 'Is there anyone special in yours?'

He simply smiled infuriatingly. 'I'll take that as a no. I'm sure if there were someone you would not be so coy.' He leaned towards her, elbows on the table. 'That happily brings me to the point of this evening. And it's so much simpler now that I know that you have no romantic encumbrances.'

Angela felt her heart give an anxious flutter. So, there had been a point to this evening, after all. She might have known it was more than just an innocent inconvenience.

His eyes skimmed her face, lightly, almost teasingly. 'Don't you want to know what this little dinner's all about?'

Angela took a deep breath. 'I have a feeling I don't, but no doubt you plan to tell me anyway.'

He smiled mysteriously, took a mouthful of his whiting and chewed thoughtfully for a moment, his dark eyes watching her. 'I need you to do me a favour, a very special favour,' he told her at last, laying down his fork.

Angela grimaced. 'And do I have the right to refuse?'

He shrugged. 'Of course you have the right. I'm not planning to clap you in irons and physically force you. But you must of course understand...' he took another mouthful of whiting '...that, if you refuse to co-operate, I shall consider our agreement broken. And, alas...' he sighed an eloquent sigh '...alas, that can have only one consequence—that you'll be forced to say farewell to Ace Personnel.'

How sweetly this man threatened. He had not even raised his voice. Indeed, the smile had never left his lips.

Angela shivered inwardly as she looked back across the table at him. 'The choice you offer is most generous,' she told him. 'And what is this favour you want me to do for you?'

Max smiled and unhurriedly laid down his cutlery, pausing before answering, enjoying her discomfort. 'I want you to come away for the weekend with me. But not as my secretary; as my lover.'

CHAPTER FIVE

ANGELA grimaced across the table at Max. 'I hate it when you make jokes,' she observed thinly. 'You have such an appalling sense of humour.'

'That wasn't a joke.' Max carried on eating.

'In that case, I must have misunderstood what you said.'

'I doubt it.' He waved a hand at her snails. 'Eat up, my dear Angela. They'll be getting cold.' Then, when she continued to scowl across at him in silence, he added, 'What I said was perfectly straightforward and simple. I want you for my lover this coming weekend.'

You had to hand it to him, when it came to sheer arrogance, Max Fielding was in a class of his own.

Angela continued to regard him narrowly. Needless to say, she had not touched her snails. 'Straightforward and simple. Is that what you call it? Personally, I would call it something else.'

'I must say, you don't appear enthralled by the idea.' Max helped himself to more whiting and smiled.

'Enthralled? Quite frankly, I'm disgusted by the idea. Where do you find the nerve even to make such a suggestion?'

Max raised his eyebrows, as though in surprise. A smile of amusement touched his dark eyes. 'Oh, did I forget to mention...?' He chewed thoughtfully for a moment. 'You won't be required to be my lover in any real sense. All I require of you is that you pretend to be.' He shook his head. 'Come, come, my dear Angela. Surely you didn't seriously imagine that I would even dream of making such a scandalous suggestion?'

So, he had tricked her. Again. Angela scowled back at him. 'I can't say I fancy the idea of pretending any better. In fact, if I was truthful, I would have to say that I find it positively repulsive.'

He smiled. 'Feel free to be as truthful as you like. Honesty is a quality I've always admired.'

'But never felt moved to aspire to,' she shot back at him. Then, when his smile merely broadened at the insult, she picked up her cutlery, extricated a snail and chewed on it angrily for a moment. Then, as he continued to watch her with amusement, she demanded, 'So, what's this silly charade you're expecting me to take part in? I suppose, since I have very little choice but to go along with it, I may as well know what it's all about.'

Max leaned back in his chair and toyed idly with his wine glass. 'Don't take it all so seriously, my dear Angela. The whole thing, I suspect, if approached in the right frame of mind, could prove to be a fairly harmless bit of fun.'

'Fun?' Her tone was leaden.

'Yes, fun, my dear Angela. You must learn to be a little less suspicious of me all the time.'

'Next, you'll be suggesting that I sprout wings and fly—but some things, Mr Fielding, I'm afraid are just not possible.'

He smiled at that. 'Don't be such a pessimist. You can't tell what's possible until you try.'

'Well, here's something *you* can try.' Angela leaned towards him. 'Try explaining what this ridiculous proposal of yours is all about.'

Max waited till the waiter had cleared away their plates. 'Have you ever been to Gloucestershire?' he queried.

Angela shook her head impatiently. Was this supposed to be an explanation? 'No, as a matter of fact, I haven't,' she answered crisply.

'Then you're in for a treat.' He poured them both more wine. 'It's a particularly pretty corner of England. Lane Park, where we'll be staying, is right out in the country. It's a big old country farmhouse surrounded by woods and fields.'

Angela grimaced in response. 'How idyllic,' she said with sarcasm. 'A positive little paradise. I can scarcely wait.'

'That's much the way I feel.' Her sarcasm simply amused him. 'I'm glad you're responding with such enthusiasm. It would be a terrible waste to take someone who didn't appreciate it.'

She had accused him earlier of having an appalling sense of humour. But it was not so much appalling as utterly maddening. Though what she had said about hating it when he made jokes remained true—not because she didn't find them funny, but for another, far more unsettling reason.

His maddening sense of humour had the ability to disarm her. He seemed almost human when he was being humorous. Human, and quite alarmingly attractive.

She squashed that thought firmly and looked him in the eye. 'That prompts me to ask the obvious question... Why aren't you taking one of your countless ladyfriends? Why on earth have I been singled out for this honour?'

'I'm glad you're suitably flattered.' He glanced down at his plate as the waiter laid their steaks before them. Then he glanced up again at Angela and continued, 'There'll be several other guests at Lane Park as well as us, so, to some extent, I'm afraid you'll have to share me.' He smiled amusedly at the grimace that provoked. 'But don't worry. I'll do my best to devote as much attention to you as befits your status as my fiancée.'

'Finacée?' Angela's eyes widened like saucers. 'Why the sudden promotion?' she queried. 'I understood I was simply to be your make-believe lover?'

'Is that what you would prefer?'

'Frankly, I would prefer neither. Frankly, I would prefer that you took someone else.'

'Perhaps that's precisely why I'm taking you. If I were to take one of my ladyfriends, as you so quaintly call them, there's the danger that they might get the wrong idea. They might decide they rather like being my fiancée and start making waves once the weekend's over.'

'Such vanity!' Angela scoffed, though she could see he had a point. To anyone too blind to see all his faults Max Fielding could be considered a pretty good catch. He was rich, he was good-looking, he had bags of sex appeal—and when he wanted he could be lethally charming. To some, an irresistible combination.

Thank heavens, she thought, though at times he can disturb me, I am still in possession of adequate vision. Beneath the shining façade I can still see, all too clearly, the cold-hearted manipulator underneath.

She assured him now, 'But you're right, you're safe with me. One of the few things I can think of that would actually be more disagreeable than pretending to be your fiancée is the thought of being your fiancée for real.' She smiled sarcastically. 'All things considered, in my opinion, that would be a fate worse than death.'

'You really think so?' His eyes twinkled with amusement. Was there nothing she could say, Angela thought with irritation, that could dent that insufferable ego of his?

It seemed not as he added, leaning back in his seat, 'By the end of the weekend you may have changed your tune somewhat.' He surveyed her for a moment through amused dark eyes in whose depths burned a flicker of overt sexual challenge. 'Undoubtedly, you will have got to know me rather better—and to have grown more appreciative of my many virtues.'

'I wouldn't count on it,' Angela advised him. Then she added evasively, glancing down at her own steak—that intimate look in his eyes, for some reason, had caused her heart to shift strangely inside her...alarm, she assured herself—'Besides, I haven't actually agreed to co-operate.'

'You will, sweet Angela, You're the sensible sort. You know it's not worth trying to thwart me.'

But what a pleasure it would be if only she dared to, if only she didn't know that he would keep his promise to close down her agency and ruin her career.

She responded with a show of defiance. 'Why should I agree when you haven't even told me what the point is supposed to be of this whole silly enterprise? There has to be some reason for you taking me along as your fiancée. I don't flatter myself that it's for the pleasure of my company.'

'Indeed it is not. Although, who knows...?' He let his voice trail off and flicked her a wicked smile. 'The pleasure of your company might turn out to be more than adequate recompense in itself.'

Angela ignored that. 'So, what's the reason? What's the pay-off? Knowing you, there has to be one.'

Max cut himself a piece of steak before replying, 'I think the less you know about my reasons, the better.' He glanced across at her and smiled a knowing smile. 'If I were to tell you, it might give you ideas. You might be tempted to try and sabotage my plans.'

Angela felt her spirits lift a little. So far, she had made no headway whatsoever in her efforts to discover what had happened to her father's money, and that failure was becoming increasingly depressing. But Max seemed to be suggesting that it might be within her power to reap some small revenge in the meantime.

If she could figure out why he needed a temporary fiancée, it would give her infinite pleasure, while pretending to go along with him, to throw a spanner in his carefully worked-out plans.

'Sabotage your plans?' She smiled across at him with relish. 'Would I even dream of doing such a thing?'

It was after eleven when they finally left the restaurant after what, if nothing else, had been a perfectly splendid meal. The company, at times, had grated a little, but the food and the wine had been beyond reproach.

Angela sank back into the cream leather passenger-seat as the Rolls swept silently through the deserted streets of Mayfair. She stared out of the window, her head turned away from Max, aware of the strange mood that had settled inside her.

Anger and outrage were what she ought to be feeling towards the man who was seated so composedly beside her. This charade he had embroiled her in was a scandalous imposition. She ought to be feeling incoherent with fury.

And she did feel furious, she assured herself, frowning. She could feel the prickle of anger burning her skin. But there was no denying that deep down inside, totally perversely, she was looking forward to the weekend.

It was simply the prospect of sabotaging his plans that made her feel that way, she decided hurriedly. Certainly, the appeal did not lie in the pleasure of his company.

They sped through the neon-lit centre of London, past Trafalgar Square with its lion-guarded fountains, then eastwards, heading for the road back to Cambridge, neither speaking, each lost in their own private thoughts.

Then out of the blue Max suddenly put to her, 'Tell me, how come you don't have a boyfriend?'

'Who said I didn't?' Caught unawares, she was defensive. What right had he to ask such personal questions?

'Does that mean you do?'

'What business is it of yours?'

'Absolutely none.' She felt him smile with amusement. 'But that's precisely the kind of business I find most intriguing.'

Angela shot him a look of censure. 'Then I suggest you go find someone else's business to be intrigued by. I don't intend entertaining you with details of mine.'

He was undeterred. 'What's the problem? Does running your business keep you so busy that you don't have any time for romance?' As Angela ignored him, he added provocatively, 'Or maybe you just don't like men?'

'Of course I like men. *Some* men,' she amended. 'And, since you're so curious, I did have a boyfriend—until fairly recently, in fact.'

He glanced at her curiously. 'Oh, and what happened?'

'Nothing happened. We just drifted apart.'

'I see. That's sad.' His tone was irritatingly sympathetic. 'But don't worry about it. These things sometimes happen.'

Angela bristled at the blatant condescension. How dared he assume that she was in need of his sympathy?

'It wasn't particularly sad,' she shot back at him. 'It was just one of those things. Of no very great importance.'

'What a hard woman you are.' She could feel him smiling. 'You appear to have the proverbial heart of stone.'

That was rich, coming from him! His heart was hewn out of solid granite! But, though it didn't really matter to her what he thought of her, she felt moved to slightly soften what she'd just told him with a totally unnecessary explanation.

'When I say it didn't really matter, at the time, of course, it did. But I try to be philosophical in these matters. It was evidently not intended to come to anything, so there was absolutely no point in getting upset about it.'

Of course, in truth, she had been upset. The relationship with Andy had lasted three years and all had seemed well until his job took him to the States. He'd gone off vowing that the separation wouldn't harm them and that he'd only be away for, at the most, a year. But he'd decided to stay on and gradually they'd lost touch.

By the time the relationship was finally, formally, severed, Angela had long ago stopped hurting. But it was not an episode she remembered with much pleasure and there was no reason at all for a stranger like Max Fielding to know any of these very private details.

He was not a man, she sensed, in whom to confide one's disappointments. Love and sex for him would be no more than a diversion. He would simply mock those who took their relationships seriously.

He flicked her a glance as they headed for the motorway. 'So, how long ago did all this happen?'

'Several months ago.'

'And there's been no one since? My, you are an abstemious young woman.'

It was exactly the sort of comment she'd expected, but all the same it really irked her. She narrowed her eyes at him. 'Not everyone cares to flit from love-affair to love-affair as, I've no doubt, it's your habit to do. Some of us are looking for quality, not quantity.'

'A worthy aim.' He smiled ironically. 'I wish you joy in its pursuit, dear Angela.'

More condescension! Angela scowled at him and decided to give it to him with both barrels. Let's see if he could take personal criticism as well as give it!

'Don't worry, I expect you to scoff,' she told him evenly. 'After all, that's the sort of man you are. If you were a serious sort of person, you wouldn't be needing to set up this stupid charade with a make-believe fiancée. You'd already have one. You might even have a wife.'

'Is that the way it is with serious people? Do they all have wives and fiancées?'

'I believe it's fairly normal.' Angela's tone was cutting. 'But, since you're a man who's quite clearly not cut out for any sort of emotional responsibility, it doesn't really surprise me that at your age you're still single.'

'At my age?' He laughed. 'Who am I— Methuselah?'

'Far from it, but most men are married by your age.' She threw him a harsh look. 'You must be at least thirty-six.'

'A shrewd guess, my dear Angela,' he congratulated her. 'I'll be thirty-six in two months' time. And I suppose you're right, I really ought to be married. It's almost a sin to deprive some lucky woman of a husband of such qualities as I possess.'

He continued to hold her eyes for a moment, savouring her muffled guffaw of protest. 'But, fortunately, it's a sin I can live with.'

'I doubt there are very few sins you can't live with.'

He laughed. 'That's true—of the few I've tried. But let me tell you something that may surprise you...I've come close to marriage a couple of times. Once extremely close. I was actually engaged once.'

This did indeed surprise her. 'What happened?' she demanded. 'Did your poor, benighted fiancée see through you in the end?'

He smiled, amused. 'Something like that. Or, perhaps, like you, we simply drifted apart.'

As they drove along in silence, Angela was wishing she'd been spared those few details about his personal history. All she needed to know about him was that he had cheated her father. Everything else was totally superfluous.

For these unexpected confidences made her feel uneasy. As though, against her will, she was being lured into his web. By revealing this human, fallible side of himself he seemed to be inviting her to trust him, to stop being so suspicious of him, to stop seeing him as her enemy.

Perhaps, she wondered, casting a quick glance across at him, he had, after all, guessed the real reason for her interest in him and was hoping to persuade her through clever manipulation to drop her campaign of revenge against him?

But that didn't make sense. If he knew what she was up to, in order to stop her all he had to do was fire her. And he had done the very opposite.

She frowned in confusion. It made no sense—unless he had decided that the best way of controlling her was to keep her close to him so that he could keep an eye on her.

All these useless computations were making her brain ache, and, what was more, they were getting her nowhere. It was pointless her trying to look inside his head. The man was as devious as a basketful of snakes.

At last they were approaching the outskirts of Cambridge, the familiar romantic skyline of turrets and towers that endowed the ancient city with an enduring wistful magic coming reassuringly into view in the distance.

Angela sighed and felt herself relax a little. Soon this evening's ordeal would be over.

They drove through the dark and empty streets of the city centre and drew up at last outside Denis's apartment.

'I'll see you to your door.' Before she could protest, Max had jumped up and was coming round to the passenger-door.

Angela stepped out on to the pavement. 'I assure you that's not necessary. I can see myself in without any problem.'

'Ah, but I insist.' He had taken her by the arm and was leading her across the pavement. He pushed open the front door. 'What kind of man would I be if I were to allow a defenceless young woman like yourself to make her way up to her apartment unescorted? Besides——' he smiled '—your safety and well-being happen to be of considerable importance to me. How would I manage this weekend if anything was to happen to you?'

Angela said nothing. Let him play his little game. There was absolutely no point in arguing.

With a pained look she allowed him to lead her to the lift, then to step inside with her and press the button for her floor. Then, as the doors closed, she kept her eyes averted as he leaned casually with his back against the wall.

'I trust that this weekend,' he observed, dark eyes on her, 'you're going to enter into the spirit of things? I shall be most disappointed if you don't play your part with feeling.'

Angela shrugged. She felt oddly claustrophobic, locked alone with him in this tiny enclosed space. 'I'll do my best, but don't expect too much. Playing the part of your starry-eyed fiancée, I suspect, isn't something that will exactly come naturally.'

He smiled. 'Consider it as a challenge—and, don't worry, I'll give you every assistance I can.' As she shot him a warning look he added, his tone mischievous, 'I take it you do know how fiancés behave?'

'I have some idea.' What was he getting at? She was aware of a sudden sharp tightening in her stomach.

'They have a very particular way of behaving— and it's absolutely essential that you get it right.'

The lift, it seemed to Angela, was taking forever. It had never taken so long before to reach the fourth floor.

She looked back at him. 'Do they?'

'Absolutely.'

Then, in a flash of madness, she asked the fatal question. 'I'm afraid I haven't noticed. What do they do?'

The expression in his eyes had subtly altered. His gaze was dark and intense as he looked across at her. 'For a start...' With a strange smile he was stepping towards her. 'For a start, dear Angela, they tend to do a lot of this...'

The next instant, to her horror, he had reached out to touch her, his hand moulding her shoulder, drawing her near. Then the fingers of his free hand were lacing her hair, trailing across her scalp, making her shiver.

There was a strange look in his eyes. Angela's heart was suddenly thumping. She longed to escape, to push him from her, to flee from this oppressive web in which he'd caught her.

But when in that very instant the lift doors opened, as though in answer to her prayers, she discovered that, inexplicably, she was incapable of moving. Her feet felt as though they were nailed to the floor.

Mutely, she stared back at him, heart beating frantically, as helpless as a rabbit caught in a trap.

His hand briefly released her shoulder and reached behind her to press one of the buttons on the panel by the door. The door closed again, the lift continued upwards, and, to Angela's consternation, instead of the horror she should be feeling, a thrill of fierce excitement went lancing through her.

'I had started to tell you about the habits of fiancés...' His hand slid down her back and tightened round her waist, drawing her unresisting body nearer. 'Here's just one of the things that fiancés do a lot...'

A smile touched his lips, making Angela's heart flutter. Then he was leaning towards her and she was gazing up at him, bound by the spell of him, totally mesmerised. Knowing perfectly well what was about to happen, but suddenly without the smallest desire to resist.

CHAPTER SIX

As MAX's lips brushed hers, Angela's heart slammed inside her. Every inch of her had suddenly turned to jelly. She could scarcely stand up. There was no way she could move.

His fingers caressed her spine, sending darts of electricity coursing from her scalp to the tips of her toes, and as his lips consumed her the knot in her stomach was pulling tighter and tighter, unbearably tighter, until she almost cried out from the sweet relentless agony. Every nerve-end in her body was suddenly aflame.

She felt her lips slacken as his tongue invaded her, flicking erotically against the backs of her teeth. She shuddered deliciously. This is madness, she was thinking. But it was a wonderful kind of madness. She could not resist it.

Angela was vaguely aware of the lift door reopening, of Max reaching behind her, then of the doors closing again. This could go on all night, she thought a little dazedly as she felt the lift slowly start to descend. And I wouldn't care. The thought flared recklessly, Let it go on all night. Let it never end.

His fingers tangled in her hair, sending shivers across her scalp, making her blood leap with an almost shameful longing. And as he pressed against

her she could feel his passion strong and hard
against her belly. Desire curled within her, coiling
ever tighter. Suddenly, she was finding it difficult
to breathe.

His hand slid inside the coat she was wearing.
Angela held her breath as it began to move slowly
over the thin, soft, slippery silk of her dress. Then
his hand cupped her breast, his fingers grazing the
hardened nipple, causing her to gasp out loud and
shudder.

This is madness... This is madness... The words
kept repeating, but they were a meaningless echo
inside her head. Every atom of her consciousness
was at that moment bound up with the sense of
sheer delight that was pouring through her body.

Her hands were laid flat against his chest, as
though, if only she could summon the strength, she
might belatedly push him away. But as his fingers
continued to mould and caress her, with a soft sigh
she allowed herself to fall against him, her hands
sliding to his shoulders, then twining round his
neck, reaching up to caress the thick silky hair.

The warm, sweet scent of him was in her nostrils, the heat of his body devouring her senses. She
felt her nostrils flare at the deliciousness of his
perfume. It flowed through her like a drug, awak-
ening strange passions. And the feel of him, his
hardness, his power and his warmth, were an over-
powering, irresistible torture. Each time he moved
against her she could feel her flesh melt.

And she had known it would be like this, she realised foolishly. Somehow, she had sensed he would stir her this deeply.

Her fingers trickled through his hair, loving the soft feel of it, aware of the deepening ache in her loins as his hand continued to roam over her breasts. She leaned against him. 'Oh, Max!' she murmured.

'I see you are not totally unversed, after all, in the mysteries of what fiancés get up to.' As he spoke, quite unexpectedly, his hand continued to move erotically against her. 'That is good.' He smiled into her flushed face. 'It will make for a most enjoyable weekend.'

It was the cool, amused tone in which he said it that caused Angela to gasp and pull away from him. 'Take your hands off me!' It was as though he had slapped her. 'What the hell do you think you're doing?'

'Just getting acquainted.' He was unperturbed by her outburst. His eyes roved over her, teasing her, taunting her. 'It seemed a good opportunity to get in a bit of practice. After all, we have a whole weekend of this sort of thing ahead of us.'

Angela blinked at him as hot shame flooded through her. While she'd been swept away on a tide of passion, he'd been getting in a bit of practice! What a pathetic little innocent she'd been! What an absolute fool she'd made of herself!

She pushed her hair from her face and glared at him in fury. 'We do not have a whole weekend of this sort of thing ahead of us! Let's get one thing absolutely straight. What happened just now was——'

But she got no further, for suddenly he was reaching out one hand towards her and she was jerking violently to one side in order to thwart this second barefaced onslaught.

'How dare you?' she shrieked. 'Can't you hear what I'm telling you?'

Then she bit her lip, feeling doubly foolish, as with an amused little smile he reached calmly past her and pressed one of the buttons on the panel by the door, clearly what he had intended doing all along.

As the lift doors opened briefly, then closed once more and began their final journey up to the fourth floor, Max leaned against the wall, arms folded across his chest. 'What were you saying?' he enquired smoothly. 'You seemed a little upset about something.'

Damn his composure! Angela gritted her teeth and scowled resolutely at the floor. 'I didn't say a thing,' she muttered angrily. 'Not a single thing. You must have imagined it.'

Then at last, to her relief, they had reached the fourth floor. Max stood aside to let her leave the lift ahead of him, and as she stepped out gratefully on to the landing, Angela turned abruptly to inform him before he could follow her, 'You may as well go straight back down again. The apartment's that one over in the corner. There's really no need for you to trouble yourself further.'

At that moment the sight she was most longing to see was the lift doors closing, with Max Fielding behind them.

He knew that, of course, which was precisely why he proceeded to step out on to the landing beside her. 'No trouble,' he assured her. He ushered her forward. 'I insist on seeing you safely inside.' He smiled at her wickedly. 'After all, my dear Angela, that surely is no less than my duty as your fiancé.'

Angela did not look at him. How he loved to torment her! How he loved to see her squirm! And suddenly she was shaking with so fierce an anger that she could scarcely get her key in the lock.

But at last it turned. She pushed the door open. 'Thank you, and goodnight!' she told him.

'Just a minute.' As she stepped into the hallway he quickly reached past her and switched on the light. Then he peered inside. 'All clear,' he smiled at her. 'I reckon it's safe for you to go to bed.'

Angela glared at him. 'Have you finished?' she demanded. 'Or is there anything else you need to do before you can find it in your heart to finally leave me in peace?'

'No, I don't think so.' He began to turn away. But even as Angela began to close the door, he turned round suddenly and took hold of the handle. 'You're right. After all, there is something else. Something we ought to get clear right now.'

His eyes raked her face without a trace of humour. The dark brows, as he spoke, drew slowly together.

'A few moments ago you said something to the effect that what happened in the lift back there would not be repeated.' He paused and smiled slowly, a smile that chilled her. 'In that, my dear Angela, I'm afraid you were mistaken. Quite regardless of whether either of us genuinely desires it, over the coming weekend it will happen rather a lot.'

The dark eyes narrowed, boring into her. 'And I shall expect you to play your part as my fiancée with the same degree of enthusiasm, my dear, sweet Angela, that you displayed so touchingly in our little practice session.'

He held her gaze. 'Do I make myself clear?' Then as she continued to watch him, livid with fury, from the doorway, he turned smartly on his heel. 'Goodnight. Sweet dreams.'

Throughout Friday the thought of the coming weekend hovered over Angela like threatening black wings.

How would she get through it? Inwardly, she shivered. But she had no choice. She had known that all along.

Max, she could tell, was enjoying her private anguish.

'Did you sleep well?' he had enquired on his arrival at the office that morning, pausing to bestow an amused, knowing smile. 'That's good,' he had added when she nodded curtly in answer. 'You'll need all your strength for the coming weekend.'

After that, Angela studiously avoided looking at him when he came into her office to remove files from the cupboards. But it wasn't necessary to look at him to be able to sense the smugly amused smile that adorned his hateful features as he glanced from time to time at her furiously bent head. From every pore he radiated enjoyment of her torment.

But it was more than just apprehension for the coming weekend that had twisted Angela's stomach into knots. For she was still struggling to come up with some rational explanation as to why she had succumbed to his advances in the lift.

No, not succumbed, she reproached herself sharply. There had been nothing at all passive about her response.

At the memory her stomach clenched inside her. She felt again that deep, sharp longing in her loins, the way her breath had fled from her body as he had kissed her, the hunger that had clutched at her as she had run her fingers through his hair.

Where had they come from, all those dangerous, crazy feelings? What on earth had possessed her to let go like that?

Well, he's a most attractive man, she tried to rationalise, knowing in her heart that was a pretty lame excuse. She had always known he was a most attractive man, but she'd never before felt tempted to fall into his arms! Hadn't she always said she could never fancy such a villain?

So why, last night, had all of that gone out the window? Why had she fallen, as ripe as a plum—

then been so utterly crushed to discover he was only playing with her?

Ice touched her skin. She had almost died of shame then. And no wonder, she thought, shivering. How had he put it? Getting in a bit of practice for the weekend?

It was that cynical revelation that made her apprehensive now. Over the coming weekend was she likely to be subjected to more of these cold-hearted little games of his?

More than likely, she decided. And how would she respond? She frowned at her computer. Surely that was no problem? It was unthinkable that she should drop her defences again. Besides, it could not happen. The knowledge that it was all a game to him would fill her, surely, not with desire, but with contempt.

She took a deep breath. She would get through this somehow. And, after all, it was only for a couple of days. Surely nothing too cataclysmic, she assured herself firmly, can happen in the space of forty-eight hours.

That evening, as she prepared to leave the office, Angela was starting to feel decidedly more confident about her ability to handle the next couple of days.

As Max appeared in the doorway of her little office, she glanced up with composure. 'Is there anything else? I'm just about to leave now,' she told him.

'Have you finished those letters?' He remained standing in the doorway. 'I'd like to get them in the post tonight.'

Angela lifted the pile of letters from her desk as she swung her tan leather bag over her shoulder. 'They're ready,' she told him. 'If you'd just like to sign them, I'll stop off and post them on my way home.'

'I'll sign them now.' He strode towards her desk, slipping his gold Cartier fountain-pen from his inside jacket pocket.

Angela watched as he bent to sign the sheaf of letters in that firm distinctive hand of his. And she was pleased to note that in spite of his nearness she felt none of the raw excitement of last night.

An aberration, she decided, firming her shoulders. An inexplicable aberration. That was all it had been.

But, as he straightened, her heart jumped. She had caught a drift of the cool scent of him. In an instant it had transported her back to the lift.

No, it was simply the sudden movement that had surprised her, she argued, bending quickly, as he moved away from her, to slip the letters into their envelopes. His scent and his nearness were quite incapable of affecting her.

He was seated at his desk when she stepped into his office, pushing the pile of letters into her bag.

'I'm off, then. Goodnight,' she bade him quickly, and began to head swiftly for the door.

'Goodnight, dear Angela. I'll see you in the morning—about half-past nine, as we've arranged.'

Angela nodded, avoiding his gaze, and took another step towards the door.

'I've advised you, dress-wise, of the sorts of things you'll be needing, so be sure to pack the cream of your wardrobe. None of that gaudy chorus-line stuff.'

'Of course not.' She had already taken those things to Oxfam! 'I'll bring precisely what you told me to bring.'

'Good.' He smiled and held her eyes. 'But there's one more thing I forgot to mention.'

'What's that?' Angela hesitated with one hand on the doorknob. She didn't at all like the look of that smile.

He continued to smile at her, making her flesh burn uneasily, and slowly began to rise up from his seat. 'I'd like you to pack your prettiest nightdress.'

Nightdress?

Angela blinked at him in horror, aware that the blood had flooded to her cheeks. 'I hope you're not suggesting,' she protested in a hoarse voice, 'that you and I are going to be sharing a room?'

'But of course.' He had come round to the near side of the desk and, hands in pockets, was leaning casually against it. 'We are, after all, supposed to be fiancés. In this day and age I think eyebrows would be raised if we were to do anything other than sleep in the same room.'

Angela took a deep breath and strode across the room towards him. 'I don't agree.' She was quivering with anger. How dared he suddenly spring this on her? 'And, what's more, I'm afraid I have no intention of sleeping anywhere except in a room of my own.'

Max shook his head. 'I'm afraid that's out of the question. The arrangement is that you're sleeping with me. Besides, though it's big, my friends' house is not a mansion. There is a limited number of rooms to go round.'

'Then I'll sleep in a hotel!' Angela was adamant. 'I am not, repeat, *not*, sharing a room with you!'

'What are you so afraid of?' He was smiling amusedly, his eyes travelling without mercy over her quivering, outraged form. 'As sleeping companions go, I'm told I'm quite agreeable. I don't snore or hog the bedclothes or talk in my sleep.'

'I might have known!' His humour failed to amuse her. Angela's fists were clenched angrily by her sides. 'I might have known I couldn't trust you to act decently! You know perfectly well this wasn't part of our bargain! I have every right in the world to refuse!'

'But surely you assumed we'd be sleeping together?'

'I assumed nothing of the kind or I would never have gone along with you!' She'd been naïve, but it was true. She'd taken it for granted that he was enough of a gentleman to arrange separate rooms.

He shrugged. 'Well, I'm sorry, but that's the way it is. Like it or not, we'll be sleeping together.'

'We most certainly will not!' She took another step closer. She felt like taking hold of him and throttling him. 'So, unless you're prepared to make other arrangements, you'd better just cancel this whole weekend.'

'Oh, I won't be doing that.' He straightened slowly, removing his hands from his trouser pockets. 'Too much depends on this weekend for me to cancel it just because you've developed a sudden fastidiousness about sharing a bedroom with me.'

'You can mock all you like.' Angela tilted her chin defiantly. 'But the fact remains that I won't do it!'

'Oh, yes, you will.'

'Oh, no, I won't, Mr Fielding!'

'Mr Fielding?' He smiled and lifted one dark eyebrow. 'I seem to recall it was "Max" last night.'

Angela felt the blood rush once more to her face. It was true, in a moment of reckless passion she had used his first name without even thinking. She had been rather hoping he might not have noticed— or that he would at least have the good taste not to refer to that lapse.

Vain hope, she thought bitterly. He had no taste. No taste, no feeling and no sensitivity.

He was smiling down at her with those cynical dark eyes of his. 'I asked you before, what are you afraid of?' His eyes scanned her face. 'If you're afraid I might rape you, I assure you you can dismiss all such fears from your mind. I only go where I know I'll be welcome. So you have nothing to worry about. You'll be perfectly safe.'

He reached out to cup her chin in his long, tanned fingers, softly at first, then, when she resisted, more firmly. He forced her to look up at him. 'Don't try to wriggle out of this. And don't make waves. I promise you, it's not worth your while.' He paused, looking down at her, not needing to elaborate. He was referring, of course, to his threat to close her agency.

Angela glared back at him, her heart pumping furiously. Never before had she hated anyone as much as she hated Max Fielding at that moment.

'And if you play your part well,' he continued in a teasing tone, 'when the weekend's over, I might release you from our agreement.' He held her eyes a moment. 'No promises, mind you. But from your point of view surely that possibility alone makes it worth your while to put up with such a small inconvenience?'

He released her chin. 'And who knows?' he added. 'You may find you rather enjoy sharing a bedroom with me, sweet Angela.'

Angela stepped away from him, breathing hard with emotion. 'I'd far sooner share a room with a tarantula. But it seems I have no choice, so, reluctantly, I agree. But take my word for it, I may be sleeping in the same room, but I definitely won't be sleeping in the same bed.'

He merely shrugged. 'All the more room for me.' Then he straightened. 'Now that we've got that cleared up, perhaps you'd leave me. I have work to finish.'

As he reseated himself behind his desk Angela was heading, stiff-legged, for the door.

'Be sure you're ready on time tomorrow morning,' he reminded her in that mocking, amused tone that so enraged her. 'You know how much I dislike being kept waiting.'

Then, as she yanked the door open, he added smoothly, 'And don't forget what I told you about the nightdress. Something sexy and glamorous ought to fit the bill.'

As she stormed through the door and slammed it shut behind her, he just had time to add, 'Of course, if, like me, you prefer sleeping in the buff, don't bother to bring a nightdress at all.'

CHAPTER SEVEN

'YOU'RE looking lovely.'

Max was standing on the doorstep, as, dressed in a pair of slim-cut burgundy trousers and a matching cashmere polo-neck jumper, Angela carried her case out on to the landing. He took the case from her, throwing her a wink as he did so. 'In fact, I've rarely seen you looking lovelier.'

Angela grimaced. 'Spare me the phoney compliments. We're not there yet. There's nobody to hear you.'

'Just getting in a bit of practice.' Deliberately, he held her eyes a moment. Then he added, 'Besides, they're not phoney compliments. You really are looking perfectly lovely. You make a fiancée any man in England would be proud of.'

As he turned towards the lift, Angela closed the door and followed him. Facetiously, she replied, 'Likewise, Mr Fielding. You make an extremely presentable fiancé yourself.'

'How kind of you to say so.' As the lift doors opened he stood aside to let her pass. Then, once inside the lift, he turned to face her. 'By the way, I must insist that you drop the formalities. You've done it once before and I'm sure you can do it again. I think my friends would find it a little

strange if my fiancée were to keep calling me Mr
Fielding all the time.'

Angela looked away smartly. *You've done it once
before.* He'd said it to shame her, to embarrass and
humiliate her. Would he never allow her to forget
what had happened two nights ago in this very lift?

The black Rolls was parked down below in the
street. Ever gallant, Max opened the passenger-door
for her, then deposited her bag in the cavernous
boot. Angela watched him beneath her lashes as he
came round to the driver's door, slid in alongside
her and switched on the engine.

He was dressed in a pair of light beige trousers
with a plain white shirt and tan leather jerkin that
lent him an air of unaccustomed informality—that
rather suited him, she decided. That compliment
she had paid him upstairs outside the lift, though
expressed light-heartedly, had been nevertheless
sincere. Today, though it irked her that such a
thought should even occur to her, she had to admit
he was looking even more attractive than usual.

'The journey ought to take about a couple of
hours.' He turned to her briefly as he slipped off
the hand-brake and slid the engine smoothly into
gear. 'I promised we'd be there in plenty of time
for lunch.'

'I see.' Angela nodded, still watching him closely.
There was an easygoing air about him today and a
confidence in his eyes that suggested he believed
that he could expect her full co-operation this
weekend.

She smiled to herself. Let him think it. Let him drop his guard and take her obedience for granted. He might then grow careless and accidentally reveal the purpose behind this little charade of theirs. Inwardly, she purred. Then she would know how best to go about her sabotage.

As they moved away from the pavement and headed for the main road it struck her that her plans for sabotage had a double purpose. Number one, she would thwart him, possibly seriously. The stakes in this game of his were probably quite high. He would not go to all this trouble just for peanuts.

Number two, he was bound to be furious with her, and to withdraw his tentative promise to release her. That would suit her perfectly. She did not want to be released yet. She needed more time to get into those secret files of his.

She applauded herself silently. How very fulfilling to be able to kill two birds with one stone. No wonder, indeed, that she was looking forward to the weekend!

Angela felt him glance across at her. 'What a treat to see you smiling. May I know what's behind your sudden good humour?'

You'll know soon enough! Angela turned to look at him. 'I was just thinking how lovely the weekend's going to be.'

He smiled a strange smile. 'I have no doubt it will be.' Then he added, 'By the way, try to get into the habit of calling me by name whenever you address me. Yes, Max. No, Max. That sort of thing. Fiancés tend to use each other's names a lot.'

He was dictating again! Angela scowled at him. 'Do they? Well, allow me to offer you some advice in return. I suggest you drop the "my dear Angela" in public. Anyone with half an ear can tell that it's not the tiniest bit sincere.'

'Just you wait till I start putting a bit of feeling behind it. Don't worry, once I get into my stride, there's not a single person will have the slightest doubt that I'm deeply and most sincerely in love with you.

'Oh, by the way.' He flicked open the glove box. 'You'd better wear this. The essential accessory. I wouldn't want my friends to think I was a cheap-skate.' He handed her a tiny leather jeweller's box which she knew before she opened it contained a ring. 'I had to guess your size, but I reckon it should fit.'

It fitted perfectly. Angela blinked down at it. 'Good grief!' she exclaimed. 'Are those stones real?' The diamond in the centre was as big as a duck egg, the rubies that circled it a flawless rich red.

Max eyed her. 'Would I trust you with real stones, my dear Angela, considering how well acquainted I am with your habits? Surely that would be just a trifle foolish?'

Angela flushed a little. So she'd asked a silly question. The stones were fake and that made her feel better. She would have felt most un-comfortable walking around with a veritable king's ransom dripping from her left hand.

She slipped the ring off again and replaced it in
its box. 'I'll put it on when we reach Lane Park,'
she told him. 'There's no need for me to wear it
yet.'

'Suit yourself.' He turned for a moment to look
at her. 'Do you like it?'

'It's beautiful. Yes.'

'Yes, what, my dear Angela?'

She took a deep breath. 'Yes, Max,' she offered.

'Good girl,' he smiled. 'That's much better.'

They arrived at Lane Park just after eleven-thirty
and parked the Rolls beside a row of other lim-
ousines. Several of their fellow guests had already
arrived.

Angela glanced around her at the imposing old
house set amid acres of woods and farmland. Max
had said his friends' house wasn't exactly a
mansion, but that, nevertheless, was how *she* would
have described it!

'So there you are! How lovely to see you!'

A man and a woman had appeared in the
doorway, and were hurrying down the steps to greet
them—the woman, Angela guessed, about the same
age as Max, the man perhaps a few years older.

The three of them exchanged warm, familiar
greetings. Angela sensed they had all been friends
for many years. Then Max turned to her. 'Angela,
meet your host and hostess. Janie, Alan . . . This is
my fiancée, Angela.'

'How lovely to meet you! And what a surprise!'
Janie shook her hand warmly, then cast a glance

at Max. 'We were beginning to think you'd never get married! I'm delighted you've found the right girl at last.'

Max smiled a blissful smile and slid his arm round Angela's waist. 'It took her a long time to come along, but my dear Angela was worth waiting for.'

He'd been right, he was a consummate actor. That 'my dear Angela' had had a most convincing ring. Angela allowed herself to lean lightly against him and let her eyes drift up to meet his. 'Dear Max,' she purred, 'you say the sweetest things.' She fluttered her lashes. 'And I'm so glad you waited.'

'When's the wedding?' It was Alan who asked the question. 'Are you planning to tie the knot soon?'

'Absolutely.' Max answered without hesitation. 'When you're as much in love as Angela and I are, there really isn't any point in waiting.'

Janie smiled fondly at the happy couple. 'This is absolutely the best news I've heard for ages. I look forward to receiving our invitation to the wedding.' She took Max's arm. 'Let's go inside now. I'll show you to your room. We'll be having lunch about one.'

Four abreast, they made their way to the front door, Angela flanked by Max, who was holding her hand tightly, and Alan, who proceeded to ask her if they'd had a good journey. But even as she answered, 'Excellent. No problems,' one ear was listening to the conversation next to her.

'Sir Gregory's arrived, you'll be happy to hear,' Janie was telling Max *sotto voce*.

'Oh, good. I was just about to ask if he was here yet.' Max's response was equally quiet.

'He's looking forward to meeting you and to doing some business. I don't think you could have timed this better if you'd tried.'

Angela didn't catch what Max said next, for Alan was inviting her to go ahead with him up the steps into the hall. But it didn't matter, she'd already heard enough. She was suddenly certain she knew the real reason for this visit—Max was hoping to do business with Sir Gregory. Now all she had to do was try to figure out what her role in all of this was supposed to be.

They were shown to their room with its adjoining bathroom and magnificent view out over the grounds.

'I hope you'll be comfortable.' Janie showed them round quickly, as their bags were brought up and laid by the door. 'I'll leave you alone now.' Discreetly, she withdrew. 'I'll see you downstairs when you're ready.'

At least there was one thing to be grateful for, Angela decided as the door closed behind their hostess. But before she could put what she was thinking into words, Max expressed quite the opposite opinion.

'Too bad. Twin beds.' His tone was rueful. 'I was rather hoping that there might be just one big double one.'

Angela threw him a sour smile. 'Were you really? Perhaps you were looking forward to sleeping on the floor? I can assure you, if the bed had been a double, there's no way you'd have ended up sharing it with me.'

'You think not?' He reached out and ran a finger around her jawbone. 'Alas, it looks as though we'll never know.' He smiled. 'But twin beds needn't be a problem. We can always push the two of them together.'

Angela pulled away from him. 'I'd prefer to do the opposite. I think they should be a great deal further apart. And by the way...' she threw him a scowl of annoyance '...there's no need to play the fond lover in private. I'd prefer it if you kept your hands to yourself.'

Max simply shrugged, picked up his suitcase, laid it on the nearest bed and snapped the locks open. 'Too bad, I was just getting into the swing of things.' He shot her an amused look. 'By the way, you're doing pretty well so far. Just make sure you keep it up.'

It really was important to him. Beneath his banter, she sensed that. Which simply made her all the keener to screw things up for him.

But she had no intention of betraying her intentions by proceeding to ask him suspicious questions—like what was going on between him and Sir Gregory, which was what she really wanted to know. Instead, leaning lightly against the other bed, she told him quite sincerely, 'I was rather surprised when you told your friends that we were planning to get married soon. Don't you think that was taking things a little too far?'

'No, I don't think so. It was they who brought up the subject.' As he spoke he proceeded to unpack his case, slipping things into drawers, hanging up stuff in the wardrobe. 'And I know very well that they'd have been greatly surprised if I'd told them I was planning on a protracted engagement. They know me, you see.' He shot her a glance. 'They know all about my impulsive and passionate nature.'

For some reason Angela looked hurriedly away and feigned a sudden interest in the view from the window. Just for an instant she had felt her stomach tighten. Just for an instant she had not felt totally comfortable to be alone in this strange place with an impulsive and passionate man.

Then with composure she looked back at him. 'It's your problem, of course. But pretty soon, surely, they're going to start wondering what's happened to their wedding invitation.' She threw him a hard look. 'You're going to look pretty silly.'

'Oh, no I won't. I'll tell them you deserted me, that you ran off with the milkman and pinched all my silver.' He raised an amused eyebrow. 'They'll be most sympathetic. And, of course, they'll assure me that I'm better off without you.'

What a cynic he was! He probably would do that. 'So, once you've finished using me, you plan to blacken my name?' There was an edge to her voice. 'How very typical!'

Max glanced up at her as he snapped shut his empty suitcase. 'Of course, I could always tell them the truth...' suddenly there was an edge to his voice, too '...that I discovered that you had only wormed your way into my life in order that you could spy on me.'

He was right. For a moment it had slipped her mind that her role in all this was not exactly innocent. But she faced him defiantly. 'Wouldn't they wonder why I should want to spy on you? Or do they already know about your guilty little secrets?'

He did not answer that. He gave her a long look that almost made her snatch her gaze away. Then he reached for her case and tossed it on the bed beside her. 'Unpack, if you don't mind. I want to see what you've brought with you.'

'Why, are you afraid I might have brought some of my chorus-line outfits?'

Her tone was mocking, but she was secretly grateful for the sudden change in the direction of the conversation. Just for a moment the air had become hostile and her breath had felt tight and uncomfortable in her chest.

She took a deep breath now. She had no desire to make up to him, but it would be preferable for the duration of the next couple of days, while they were forced to spend so much time in each other's company, that they behave to one another in a semi-civil manner. Otherwise, this weekend could prove to be unbearable.

He threw her a shuttered look. 'That would not have been wise. If, when you open up that case, I find those gaudy outfits in there, I'm afraid I cannot be held responsible for your safety.'

There was humour in his tone, but there was a warning in it also. 'What will you do? Strangle me with the bed sheets?' Angela looked back at him, openly taunting. She made no move to open up her case. 'Surely it wouldn't matter to you all that much?'

'Don't count on it, my dear Angela.' He had taken a step towards her. 'Now just open up the case and show me what's in there.'

Angela fiddled with the lock, deliberately tormenting him. 'Surely you wouldn't let a couple of pairs of Lurex leggings and a see-through blouse upset you excessively? I promise you, they're all the rage.'

She smiled to herself as his scowl grew darker. It made rather a pleasant change to be the one in control. Then, watching his face, she slowly pulled back the zip.

'Surprise! Surprise!' She threw the lid back.

It took only one glance for Max to realise that she had followed his instructions to the letter. There were a couple of stylish dresses, suitable for dinner, some cashmere sweaters, some skirts and silk blouses.

As she pulled them out and laid them before him, he nodded his head in obvious approval. Then, quite unexpectedly, he caught her by the wrist and twisted her round, forcing her to look up at him. He looked into her eyes. 'You enjoyed that, didn't you?'

The gesture had taken her quite by surprise. Angela blinked at him. 'What did I enjoy?'

'Playing me along like that. Spinning it all out. Keeping me in suspense for as long as possible about what you were hiding in that case.'

'But I wasn't hiding anything.'

'So I've discovered. But you wanted me to think you were.' His grip tightened a little. He drew her closer. 'Do you know what you are, my dear Angela? You are a tease.'

'I am nothing of the sort! It was just a harmless bit of fun! What's the matter? Can't you take a joke?'

She tried to tug her hand free, but he held her fast. She tried to pull away from him, but he simply pulled her closer.

'Sure, I can take a joke.' He reached out to touch her hair. 'But I must warn you that playing games can be dangerous. Such games between a man and woman can lead, as you must know, to all sorts of things.'

Angela's heart was suddenly thumping like a drum in her chest. As his fingers grazed her scalp, then brushed the contours of her face, her skin felt hot and cold, prickling with sensation. And, quite suddenly, all desire to escape him had vanished. It was shameful, but all at once she longed for him to kiss her.

But, to her surprise, he did not. All at once, he released her. 'I suggest you bear that in mind, my sweet Angela, for the remainder of the weekend. Otherwise, who's to tell what might happen?' He let his eyes drift over her, languorously, explicitly, as though he had stripped away her clothes and she was standing there naked. 'We might end up becoming lovers for real.'

'Don't worry, Mr Fielding, there's no chance of that!' Suddenly, she was desperate to put some space between them.

What had come over her? Why had she acted so foolishly? How could she ever have allowed him to get such an idea into his head?

She snatched up one of her dresses from the bed with shaky hands and darted past him to hang it in the wardrobe. She glared at him over her shoulder. 'So kindly keep your distance! I don't intend to tolerate any more of your advances! You're the last man in the world who's ever likely to become my lover!'

But as she fumbled with the coat hanger, aware of his eyes upon her, panic, like a cold fist, was closing round her heart. Would such words, such promises, be enough to protect her from a man as ruthless and cynical as Max Fielding?

And, more to the point, were they enough to protect her from the dark, secret longings she could feel inside her, uncoiling treacherously, like a snake?

CHAPTER EIGHT

'How about a walk to work off a few of those calories?'

Lunch, an informal but sumptuous affair that for the best part of three hours had kept the half-dozen guests seated happily round the table, was over at last and the guests were dispersing. One couple, along with their host and hostess, to the tennis courts to play a game of mixed doubles; Max and Angela, at the invitation of Sir Gregory, to take a stroll around the gardens with himself and his wife.

Max nodded. 'Good idea.' Then he glanced at Angela. 'How do you feel? Do you fancy a walk, darling?'

As he had said it he had slipped an arm round her waist and was gazing down at her through eyes filled with warmth and affection. Angela smiled back at him with equal insincerity. 'I'd like nothing better. It's a splendid idea.'

His lips brushed her hair. 'Perhaps you'd better change your shoes.' He glanced down with concern at the high-heeled courts she was wearing. 'We wouldn't want you to turn your ankle.' Then he winked. 'We'll wait for you out in the garden.'

What a caring, solicitous fiancé he was! He never faltered once. He really was perfect.

With a wry inner smile and a long loving look, Angela lingeringly took her leave of him. She too, she was learning, could play the part of fond lover almost as convincingly as he. 'All right. I'll only be a couple of minutes, darling.' She cast a quick smile at Sir Gregory and his wife Daphne. 'I hope you don't mind? I'll be as quick as I can.'

But as she hurried upstairs she felt certain she knew the real reason why Max wanted a few minutes alone with Sir Gregory. Over lunch, although nothing had been discussed in detail, she had figured out the nature of Max's business with Sir Gregory—and had figured out too, she was almost certain, the reason why he had brought her along to pose as his fiancée.

It had been a chance remark over the roast lamb. Sir Gregory had winked across the table at Max. 'Perhaps you and I can have a little chat some time over the next couple of days? I've been told by my City friends that you're the best man to deal with, and now that I've finally had the pleasure of meeting you, I can see that you're definitely a man after my own heart. A man with sound business flair coupled with old-fashioned family values...' He had paused and cast a quick, approving glance at Angela. 'That's the sort of man I like to deal with.'

Angela smiled to herself now as she crossed the landing to the bedroom. It was perfectly clear that the reason Max was here was in order to recruit Sir Gregory as his client, and it was equally obvious that he had needed a fiancée in order to project the required image.

Sir Gregory and his wife were definitely of the old school. They'd expect any man over thirty to be married and would tend to be suspicious of him if he wasn't. And the next best thing to being married was to appear to be imminently on the point of becoming so, with a highly visible fiancée to prove it.

So now she knew how she could sabotage the weekend. It was quite simple. All she had to do was reveal to Sir Gregory that her engagement to Max was nothing but a sham.

She pushed open the bedroom door and stepped inside. What pleasure it would give her to scupper his plans. Almost as much pleasure as she would experience on the day when she finally revealed him to be the downfall of her father.

Kicking off her shoes, Angela crossed to the wardrobe to find herself a pair of loafers. She must pick her moment carefully for her revelation, some moment when the guests were all gathered together and she could be sure of inflicting maximum damage. What a fool he was going to look in front of his friends! What a cheap liar! What a charlatan!

She stuck her feet into the loafers and gazed down at them for a moment. His friends might find the duplicity a little hard to believe. After all, he played his part so convincingly. Over lunch he had peppered his conversation with just the right number of intimate asides to her, as well as a clutch of warm glances that were perfectly rationed and a score of touches and caresses that were immaculately timed. Behaving to the letter as one would expect a man who was deeply in love to behave.

And at times, she had to confess, it had felt a little odd, being the object of so much affection. It had even crossed her mind that if it were genuine, if all that attention and consideration had been directed at someone he truly loved, that person would indeed be lucky. For in a silly sort of way he had actually made her feel as though she were the most special, most desirable woman in the world.

Not many men could make a woman feel like that. Certainly none that she had ever met.

And that, she told herself, giving herself a firm mental shake, simply made his deception all the more contemptible. Any man to whom deceit and lies came so easily quite simply deserved everything he got.

In the meantime... She stood up and squared her shoulders. In the meantime, she would enjoy their little stroll around the gardens. And he would never suspect what she was plotting!

With a smile on her lips she hurried downstairs.

The gardens were exquisite—stretches of bright autumn flowerbeds and manicured green lawns with fountains playing.

'Isn't this delightful?' Daphne smiled appreciatively at Angela as the two women followed a few paces behind the men, who, judging from the snatches of conversation that Angela had overheard, were discussing in some detail the investment possibilities of the money Sir Gregory was planning to entrust to Max.

She wished she could have heard more, but she was trying to be discreet. She returned the smile of the older woman. 'It's absolutely beautiful,' she agreed in all truth.

And then they turned a corner and came upon a maze, whose green privet hedges towered above their heads.

'Let's go through it!' It was Daphne's idea. 'I haven't been through a maze in years!' Then she smiled mischievously at the others. 'Let's play a game! Max and Angela can set off in one direction and Gregory and I will set off in the other, and we'll see which couple finds their way out first!'

Angela felt less than enthralled by that idea. Just the thought of wandering round a maze with Max made her feel distinctly claustrophobic. She looked at Max, quietly confident that he could be relied on to come up with some excuse—for surely the idea must appeal to him no more than it did to her?

But instead, 'You're on,' he responded, smiling. 'And, just to make it a little more interesting . . . the last couple back at the house for tea owes the other couple a bottle of champagne.'

Daphne smiled knowingly and winked at her husband. 'I think we're in for a bottle of champagne. These two lovebirds, if I'm not mistaken, will be in no hurry whatsoever to extricate themselves from the maze.'

This piece of romantic fiction seemed to appeal to Sir Gregory. He winked at Max. 'Can't say I blame you. If I were twenty years younger and had a beautiful fiancée like yours I wouldn't mind at all getting trapped in there all night!'

Angela scowled at Max as the others set off and they themselves turned off in the opposite direction. 'What did you do that for? Why did you encourage them to make a silly contest of this?'

'Why not? It's just supposed to be a bit of fun. What are you worried about? Are you afraid we might get lost?'

Angela pulled a face. 'Isn't that what we're supposed to do? Pretend to get lost so they can think we're up to something and have a good giggle behind our backs?'

Max shrugged as they rounded a narrow corner. 'I don't mind them giggling. There's no harm in it.' He caught her eye. 'And they'll be wrong, anyway, won't they?' He raised one dark eyebrow. 'We won't be getting up to anything.'

'Definitely not.' Angela stepped away from him, feeling increasingly uneasy about being alone with him in this dark, secret place. With each step they took the hedges seemed to close in on them, squeezing them together in an ever-more tiny space.

Defensively, she clasped her arms around her chest. 'And, since neither of us really wants to be here, I suggest we make for the exit as quickly as we can.'

'All in good time. There's no hurry, my dear Angela. Remember, we have an image to keep up.'

Angela turned to look at him, mild horror in her face. 'Don't tell me you seriously intend to hang about in here just in order to keep up our image?'

'Just for half an hour. Then we can make our way out—and, whether or not we make it before Daphne and Gregory, at least our honour as lovers will remain intact.'

'Oh, no! I'm not hanging around in here for half an hour! I don't care a damn about our honour as lovers! I'm sick of this whole ridiculous sham, anyway!'

So saying, she dived into a nearby opening, made a sharp right turn and dived down another one. 'I'll just say I lost you!' she called over the hedge. 'Don't worry, I'll pretend to be broken-hearted!'

'That won't be necessary.' To her consternation, as she zigzagged swiftly through another opening, suddenly Max was standing right in front of her.

She gasped up at him disbelievingly. How on earth had he done that? And through her annoyance she was aware of a tiny spark of admiration. Never before had she met a man who managed with such apparent ease to keep one jump ahead of her all the time.

He answered her unspoken question with a smile. 'I happen to know this maze rather well. This isn't the first time I've been through it.'

'Then tell me how to get out of it!' She raised her head to challenge him, aware that her heart was beating strangely inside her. He was standing so close that his shadow loomed over her, seeming to wrap around her like a blanket, imprisoning her within its folds.

It was a feeling he frequently instilled in her, it occurred to her. This feeling of being trapped, caught in his power. And she did not like it, especially now, when to all effects she really was trapped and at his mercy.

She cleared her throat when he did not answer but simply stared down at her with those iron-grey eyes of his that at times could pierce right through her like bayonets, but now seemed like endless, deep, dark pools, drawing her into their inky blackness.

Then he spoke. 'I could get us out of here in two minutes.' Then he smiled strangely. 'That is, if I wanted to.'

'Then do it. Please.' Her voice was unsteady. Suddenly she seemed unable to control her breathing. 'I don't want to stay in here. There's no point. It's silly. If you like, we can go and hide somewhere else for half an hour. Somewhere out in the garden. Then they won't be disappointed and they'll win their champagne.'

He smiled at that. 'What a little trickster you are. Don't you have any scruples, my dear Angela?' He reached out and touched her cheek with his finger, making her flesh jump, making her heart scream.

'No, I couldn't possibly agree to that.' As he spoke, his gaze continued to spill into hers, so that she had to close her eyes to stop herself from drowning. 'But I'll tell you what we can do...' His finger traced her jaw. Then, as it came up to brush her mouth, she felt her lips part. 'Since you feel so sure that you can find your way out of here, you lead us out. Where you go, I'll follow.'

He had spoken those last words like a lover's promise. In two simultaneous but quite separate reactions, Angela felt her heart squeeze and jerked her head away from him. His choice of words no doubt had been intended to mock their current farcical situation. But at the same time, she sensed, feeling a strange stab inside her, more directly, they had been intended as a mockery of her.

Was he aware of the mesmeric effect he sometimes had on her? The thought appalled her. Deliberately, she scowled at him.

'OK, if that's the deal, I'll go along with it.' She turned her back on him and marched through the nearest opening. 'This maze, after all, isn't terribly big. It shouldn't take me long to find my way out of it.'

Brave words. It was more than an hour later before they finally emerged. She would have been wiser simply to have played along with him. That way they would have been out in half the time.

'I'll bet you enjoyed that!' She glared at Max as they made their way back through the garden. She was feeling hot and bothered and thoroughly frustrated. At one point it had seemed they might never see the exit! And Max, needless to say, had done nothing to help her.

'It had its moments.' His tone was amused now. 'When we arrived back at the centre for the third time I half expected you to start tearing down the hedges.'

'Believe me, I was tempted.' Angela scowled at him. Though first, she might have added, before I started on the hedges, it would have given me the greatest pleasure to start demolishing you!

But attention in that instant was diverted. As they rounded a sudden bend and began to approach the house, a burst of spontaneous applause greeted them from the terrace.

'Here they come at last!' someone shouted. Then Sir Gregory's voice boomed, 'Mr Fielding, Daphne and I are looking forward to that champagne!'

What a ridiculous farce! Angela scowled bad-temperedly. And she almost pulled away as Max leaned towards her and tucked her arm affectionately through his.

'Smile!' he commanded in a whisper. 'Look as though you enjoyed our little sojourn in the maze.' He drew her a little closer and for the benefit of the crowd ruffled her hair and kissed her nose. 'Try to look like a woman in love,' he murmured. 'Glow a little. Walk on air. And, remember, every single one of them envies us. All the world loves, and envies, a lover.'

Angela rose to the occasion and tilted her face to gaze at him. 'Will this do?' she muttered between clenched teeth. 'Am I glowing sufficiently for you?'

He kissed her check. 'You're glowing beautifully. And your audience is absolutely loving it.'

Angela smiled inwardly. Not as much, she was thinking, as they're going to love hearing what I have to tell them about you!

It was at dinner that evening that Angela took her chance to spill the beans about their fake engagement.

For some reason, in spite of all the aggravations of the day, she was feeling in a positively buoyant frame of mind—though that was really quite easily explained, she decided. Janie and Alan, and their fellow guests, were wonderful, entertaining company, and Lane Park itself was an enchanting place to be.

But in addition, she was discovering, this charade of hers and Max's, as he had predicted at the beginning, was at times a lot of fun. He seemed to be enjoying it and his enjoyment was infectious.

Though this sense of collaboration could be dangerous, she realised. It could lull her into a false sense of acceptance. Which was all the more reason for her to play her hand against him before her resistance to him became perilously eroded.

At the first opportunity, she had decided, she must strike.

Angela had chosen to wear the red sheath dress to dinner, and she'd swept back her hair with a pair of *diamanté* combs in a style that was chic, but softly flattering. She seated herself at the circular mahogany table, set with twinkling silver and delicately cut crystal, Max at her side, dressed in a formal dark suit and, to her mild irritation, that same red tie that matched so perfectly the colour of her dress.

And, knowing the treachery she was soon to spring on him, she was enjoying more than usual the attention he was paying her. She smiled into his face as he handed her her napkin. 'Thank you, darling.' She lowered her lashes coyly. Then she reached across in front of him to pick up his napkin, shook it loose and laid it fondly over his lap. 'There you are, my sweetness,' she murmured lovingly.

But, as their eyes met, he smiled. 'Thank you, my sweet Angela.' Then before she had time to withdraw her hand he had caught hold of it tightly and pressed her palm against his thigh.

It was only for the briefest of instants, but in that instant the colour rushed to her cheeks. The feel of the hard-muscled flesh beneath her fingers had caused her heart to skip a beat.

Momentarily the boundaries between pretence and reality had become worryingly, threateningly, fuzzy and blurred. The jolt that had gone through her had been no make-believe. The raw ragged echo of it reverberated still.

Once more, all too clearly, she had been reminded of the dangerous nature of the game she was playing.

He still held her hand lightly between his fingers. As she glanced away hurriedly she could feel his eyes watching her, eyes that she sensed were bright with amusement. No one else knew it, but he was quietly laughing at her.

Just wait! she vowed. Before this meal is over I'll have wiped that smug smile from your face!

Her moment came during dessert, a delicious chocolate pudding, laced with kirsch and brandy, and served with lashings of whipped cream. And it was Sir Gregory, appropriately, who provided her opening.

'I always think of chocolate pudding,' he told the table amiably, casting a swift, meaningful glance in Max and Angela's direction, 'as being the special pudding of lovers. I remember Daphne's parents served us chocolate pudding on the day I asked her to be my wife.'

There were one or two approving murmurs round the table. 'How romantic,' someone said.

'And how appropriate,' cooed someone else, 'that our hostess should have chosen to serve it this evening when Max and Angela are with us.'

Max smiled politely. 'We'll remember that, Sir Gregory.' Then he cast a devoted glance at Angela. 'From now on every time we have chocolate pudding we'll remember this evening, won't we, darling?'

We shall indeed! Angela gazed fondly back at him, secretly savouring the moment before she pounced. Then she took a deep breath and swivelled round to address the others, letting her gaze rest finally on Sir Gregory.

'You know, Max and I aren't really in love. The engagement, the ring...' she waved her left hand '...the whole thing, I'm sorry to say, is a sham.'

CHAPTER NINE

Two things happened simultaneously. Sir Gregory's eyebrows soared to the top of his forehead and Angela received a sharp stab in the ankle from the toe of Max's shoe.

She gasped as in a smooth tone she heard Max say, his hand reaching for hers and raising it to his lips with a tenderness that was in positively breath-taking contrast to the distinctly more violent goings-on out of sight beneath the table, 'You see, she's not only beautiful, but she also has a sense of humour. Though I can assure you, my dear Angela . . .' he smiled into her eyes '. . . I can assure you that there's nothing sham about that ring you're wearing.'

'I'll say!' Across the table, Sir Gregory boomed with laughter. 'And you can't fool me, young lady,' he warned her. 'I know a young couple in love when I see one.'

'You were joking, weren't you?' Max leaned towards Angela, amusing his audience by making a show of concern. 'You'd better tell me now, publicly, if the engagement is off.'

As he spoke, his foot curled round her ankle, so tightly that her own foot was rapidly becoming numb. Angela gritted her teeth. He was playing this beautifully. There was not a person in the room who believed what she'd just told them.

'If that's what you call not being in love...' Janie was laughing as she said it '...I'd enjoy seeing what you two would be like if you really did love one another!'

Max had laced his long strong fingers with Angela's, resting them lightly on the table. 'Come on, out with it,' he encouraged with a half-smile, softly kissing the back of her hand. 'We're all still waiting for your answer. Don't you love me any more? Is the engagement really off?' As he spoke his tone was light and bantering, the tone of a man who had nothing to fear.

This was not how Angela had expected things to go. She had contrived it badly. She felt an utter fool.

She looked back at Max, aware of all eyes on her—and aware, too, of the lethal foot beneath the table that continued to hold her own foot captive. If she said the wrong thing, she had a very strong suspicion, he might snap her foot off at the ankle.

With difficulty, she smiled at him. 'My dear Max, I was only teasing. Surely you know how I feel about you?'

'I'll drink to that!' Sir Gregory raised his wine glass. He beamed. 'A toast to the happy couple.' Then, as the other guests followed his example and glasses clinked merrily round the table, he winked across at Max and added in a low voice, 'To the happy couple—and, of course, to our agreement!'

As conversation resumed, Max released her aching ankle, but before Angela could reach down to rub it back to life he had caught hold of her hand and was twisting her round to look at him.

He was smiling, but there was a dark look in his eyes and the fingers around her wrist bit into her like handcuffs.

'Don't think this is finished,' he warned her in a low voice. 'We shall resume this later in the privacy of our room.'

The meal ended much too quickly for Angela's liking.

For one thing, as the cigars and brandy were handed round, the atmosphere around the table became positively jovial. And Angela found herself putting her private dilemmas behind her and joining whole-heartedly in the fun of it all. It felt like a long time since she had enjoyed herself so much.

And to a large extent the cause of her enjoyment—and, indeed, of the whole table's—was undoubtedly Max. Never before had she seen him so easy and relaxed, nor suspected he was such a witty raconteur.

Forgetting how much she hated him, she listened with delight as he spun story after story to his mesmerised audience. She even found herself idiotically enjoying the envious glances of the other women round the table. There was not one of them, she sensed, who did not envy her her position as bedmate and future wife and companion of the brightest, sexiest man in the room!

It was only when, at last, the guests rose from the table and began to bid one another goodnight that Angela remembered the other reason why she had been so reluctant for the evening to end.

After that angry warning he had issued, she was not relishing in the slightest being alone with Max.

Though perhaps, she wondered, as they made their way upstairs, he had forgotten his anger and his threat. She prayed that he had. She did not want him to be angry. That would spoil what had been a near-perfect evening.

He said nothing as they reached the top of the stairs and he proceeded to lead her along the corridor to their room. And she was still hopeful as he pushed the bedroom door open and invited her to step inside.

Then the door closed softly and very slowly he turned to face her, and in an instant she saw all her hopes turned to dust.

For a moment he said nothing, just let his eyes bore through her. Then in a low voice he accused her, 'That was a damned stupid trick. What did you have to go and do a stupid thing like that for?'

'Because I wanted to.' It was a stupid, childish answer, but in the sudden rush of disappointment that, irretrievably now, the evening was ruined, it was the only answer she could think of.

His gaze was shuttered, his expression unreadable. 'And why did you want to? What was the purpose?' He frowned at her suddenly. 'Were you drunk or something?'

'No, I wasn't drunk. I've never been more sober. I'd been planning to do it even before we came here.'

'I see.' His dark eyes surveyed her for a moment. 'But I still can't see what made you do it. To get back at me—I can see that part of it—but in the long run it wasn't really in your interests.'

'You're wrong. It was very much in my interests. You've no idea how much I would have enjoyed seeing you revealed in front of all your fine friends for the despicable phoney that you are!'

Max surprised her by smiling. 'Oh, I'm well aware of that. And no doubt it would also have greatly warmed the cockles of your spiteful little heart to sabotage my agreement with Sir Gregory. As you were obviously astute enough to gather, he likes the people he deals with to be like him—respectably married family men.

'But, surely...' his eyes narrowed '...surely your first consideration ought to have been the possibility of my releasing you if you played along with me this weekend? After all, I seem to recall you lamenting the fact that I was preventing you from getting on with the running of your business.

'What's the matter?' He smiled at her strangely. 'Have you developed, after all, a sudden taste for working for me?'

'Don't flatter yourself.' Angela glanced away awkwardly. Then, thinking quickly, she narrowed her eyes at him. 'I simply didn't believe you would release me,' she told him. 'I hope you don't think

I'm such a fool as to take anything you might say as gospel?'

'And I, my dear Angela, am not quite the fool that you apparently believe me to be.' He smiled a scathing smile. 'Did you seriously imagine that I would let you get away with that foolish little outburst?'

Not get away with it, exactly. She had expected some kind of retaliation. But what she had definitely not been expecting was that he would handle such a tricky situation so deftly.

And that made her the fool, she suddenly realised as she looked back into his clever, ruthless face. She ought to know by now that this man before her was capable of manoeuvring his way out of anything.

She shrugged a little foolishly. 'Well, it doesn't really matter what I did or didn't imagine. My attempt to expose you fell flat on its face. You won. That should be enough to please you.'

'Should it?' He seemed to examine her for a moment, then with a shake of his head he turned away. 'This may come as a surprise to you, but I found nothing at all pleasing about this evening's little episode.'

As Angela looked at him, she felt oddly chastened. She, too, was half wishing she'd left well alone. Not only had her action spoiled an otherwise happy evening, but if she was strictly honest she had to admit that there was a part of her that was uneasy with what she'd done. It had been spiteful and underhand and not at all like her. And the way he'd just looked at her, more with disappointment than with anger, had caused that uneasiness to sharpen.

He hadn't deserved it, she thought illogically. And yet that was crazy. Inexcusable. Why should she feel guilty about her attempt to betray him? Surely, that was *precisely* what he deserved?

As she continued to look at him, confused and guilty, his expression altered. He smiled unexpectedly.

'Let's forget it. It's over. And it won't happen again.' He held her eyes a moment. 'Will it, dear Angela?'

As she glared at the floor, he continued, 'Besides, it's time for bed and I'm rather tired.'

As he said it he slipped off his charcoal-grey jacket and loosened the brilliant red tie at his throat. 'Since I'm a gentleman, I'll let you use the bathroom first, then you can be all safely tucked up in bed by the time I come to join you.'

Angela's eyebrows shot up. 'Before you *what*?'

'Join you, my dear Angela—but only in a manner of speaking.' Suddenly, there was amusement dancing in his eyes. 'Don't worry, I don't plan on climbing into bed with you.' He tossed his jacket and tie on to one of the chairs, then frowned for a moment as he regarded the twin beds. 'I think you were right, we ought to move them apart. They're really much too close for comfort. I'll do that while you're getting ready.' He nodded towards the bathroom. 'Go ahead,' he told her.

By the time Angela emerged warily from the bathroom, clad in a demure broderie anglaise nightdress that covered her from her throat to her ankles, the beds had been moved to opposite sides of the room, the two gilt chairs placed like a barrier between them.

Max regarded her and smiled. 'Quite pretty, if a little virginal. What happened to the sexy nightdress I ordered?'

Angela crossed to the bed in the corner by the window. 'I must have unaccountably forgotten it,' she retorted. 'How very disappointing for you.'

He shrugged. 'But less disappointing than I'd expected. I was fully prepared for you to turn up with a pair of passion-killing winceyette pyjamas.'

Angela cut him a glance across her shoulder. 'I wish I'd known that was your pet aversion. I would've gone out and bought a pair.'

'I believe you would.' He smiled at that. 'And, if you had, I would simply have had to pray that there wasn't a fire in the middle of the night. If my fiancée was to be caught wearing old ladies' pyjamas, I'm sure my friends would be seriously worried about my sex life.'

As Angela touched the high neck of her nightdress, he continued to survey her for a moment. 'As it is, what you're wearing isn't much better. Not really the sort of thing a woman normally chooses for a romantic weekend with her lover.'

For some reason that irked her. 'No doubt you're an expert?' She glared at him, waiting for his answer.

But Max simply smiled. 'However,' he told her, 'I suspect you'll end up shedding it before the night's done.' As her cheeks flamed with colour, wondering what he was hinting, he held her eyes a moment, then added, turning away towards the bathroom, 'I think you'll find it much too hot.'

By the time Max re-emerged from the bathroom, Angela was indeed tucked up in bed, the covers pulled right up to her chin. Pretending to be asleep, she lay on her side and watched him surreptitiously from between her lashes.

He was clad only in the bottoms of a pair of silk pyjamas—that threat about preferring to sleep in the buff had evidently been intended to alarm her!—and as he proceeded to hang up his suit in the wardrobe she longed to close her eyes and feign indifference to the broad, suntanned back and well-muscled shoulders.

But she could not close her eyes. She felt totally mesmerised by the startlingly virile perfection of him. Deep inside her, deliciously, a pulse began to beat. She longed to slip from her bed and embrace him.

Shameless idiot! She snapped her eyes shut, then opened them slowly, controlling her breathing, as he shut the wardrobe door and turned for a moment to cast a glance in her direction.

He had felt her watching him! Anxiously, her heart leapt. She closed her eyes tightly and stopped breathing altogether.

Then a moment later she heard him switch the light off, plunging the room into instant darkness.

But she continued to hold her breath until he had climbed into bed and the only sound that filled the room was the fierce, chaotic beat of her heart.

To her astonishment Angela drifted off to sleep quite quickly. But just a couple of hours later she awoke with a start, as wide awake as though it were morning.

She stared into the darkness, her heart beating strangely. She'd been awakened by a dream and the dream still clung to her. Its vivid, bright colours seemed to dance all around her. Its message was written in letters of fire before her eyes.

With a frown she drew herself up against the pillows. The revelation she had dreamed, she suddenly realised, was an idea that had been taking shape inside her head all day. But it had taken the mysterious powers of the unconscious to lay it before her in clear, simple terms.

She closed her eyes and listened for a moment to the quiet, regular breathing on the other side of the room. Max, she was suddenly certain, hadn't stolen from her father. She'd been wrong about that. He wasn't to blame.

With a sigh she pushed the bedcovers down from her shoulders, feeling suddenly uncomfortably sticky and damp. He'd been perfectly right, this nightdress was too hot. Before she slept again she would need a shower.

She slipped silently from the bed and crossed to the bathroom, casting a quick glance at Max's sleeping form. She should have known all along.

The evidence had been right in front of her, if only she'd taken the time to examine it. Instead, she'd stuck to her conviction and stubbornly ignored it.

The bathroom door opened without a sound. Angela slipped inside and switched on the light. With a sigh she stripped off and stepped under the shower, turned on the cold tap and let the water sluice over her.

What a fool she'd been. What a blind, blinkered fool. She had simply believed what she'd wanted to believe. She grabbed a towel and rubbed herself vigorously. How could she have failed to see the truth?

It had been this afternoon when they'd been walking with Sir Gregory that the suspicion that she was mistaken had started to dawn on her. Just a snatch here and there of his private chat with Max had been enough to plant the unconscious doubts in her mind.

She pulled on her nightdress and pushed back her hair. Added to all the other bits of information that she had so single-mindedly ignored, what she had heard today had finally convinced her of the terrible mistake that she had made.

And now she had to speak to him, she had to explain. Above all, she thought, she had to apologise.

As she pushed open the bathroom door a shaft of light fell across the sleeping figure in the bed. She saw him stir, then he opened his eyes. 'Angela? Is something wrong?'

Angela felt her heart squeeze inside her. She longed to go to him, to get down on her knees and at last explain to him the guilty muddle in her head. To tell him she was sorry, to drown in his forgiveness. To melt into the embrace of those strong naked arms.

He was half sitting up now, propped on one elbow, and he was squinting into the light that flooded from the bathroom. 'Angela, are you all right?' He began to sit up. 'What's the matter? What are you doing there?'

As Angela looked at him she felt a shudder go through her and a longing that almost tore her in two.

She clenched her fists tightly, fighting for control, squeezed her eyes closed and took a deep calming breath.

Not now. She could not go to him now. To go to him now, she knew, would be madness.

She took another deep breath. 'Go back to sleep, Max. Nothing's wrong. I needed a drink, that's all.'

Before he could answer, she had switched off the light and on legs of rubber was hurrying back to bed.

Later, she promised herself, I'll tell him in the morning. When I'm feeling myself again. When I have recovered my senses.

She pressed her face into the pillow, shivering with excitement, her brain on fire. This changes everything, she kept thinking, her pulses racing. I no longer have to hate him. I no longer have to fear him. Max is not my enemy. Had I but known it, he never was.

And suddenly, though she dared not put a name to them, the world seemed full of the most wonderful possibilities.

CHAPTER TEN

NEXT day, to Angela's growing frustration, by mid-afternoon she had still not had a chance to reveal to Max the secret that consumed her.

Over breakfast with the other guests she watched him beneath her lashes, her blood surging joyfully with the new knowledge that he was not, after all, the villain she had believed.

As he caught her eye and smiled across the table at her, she snatched away her gaze and tried to calm her beating heart. She was being foolish. Reckless. Completely crazy. Her revelation, when considered in the cold light of day, actually changed very little at all. The only real difference was that she finally knew the truth.

A pain stabbed through her. It was quite unrealistic to hope for or dream of anything more.

On a wave of realism she sought to distance herself from her crazy imaginings of the night before. Why on earth should it matter to her so desperately that Max was not the trickster she had supposed? In truth, all her discovery actually meant was that she had wasted her time utterly in pursuing him—and that she was no further forward in her quest to discover what had happened to her father's money.

And when she finally had the chance to tell him of her discovery, there would be no tears or embraces of reconciliation. He would not fling his arms abandonedly around her, as in her crazed state last night she had secretly fantasised.

Nor would I even want him to, she told herself firmly. Heaven knows what I was thinking of. I must have been mad.

But all the same, she had to speak to him. She had to explain and apologise—in a sane, controlled manner. I owe him that, she decided calmly, as, breakfast over, they left the table and moved with the others out into the garden.

How would he react to her apologies and explanations? As they sat on the veranda, glancing through the Sunday papers before heading down to the tennis courts for a game, she glanced at his dark, unheeding profile. More than likely, he would simply shrug them off. More than likely, they would matter to him hardly at all.

So be it. With a determined inner shrug, she swallowed back the jolt of disappointment inside her. They did not matter greatly to her, either. It was simply a matter of setting the record straight.

And perhaps, it occurred to her by way of compensation, once her secrets were all out in the open, Max might be able to guide her in her search to discover the truth about her father's financial downfall. After all, if there was a subject he understood, it was money. He might be able to suggest some ideas.

Having rationalised away her inner turmoil, Angela gradually began to feel calmer. By the time she and Max, along with the other guests, gathered on the patio at one o'clock for lunch, in spite of the lovers' charade they were still playing, she felt inwardly composed and comfortably detached.

When the right moment came, she would say what she had to say. In the meantime, she would think no more about it.

It was just after tea and a couple of hours before dinner that Angela finally had her chance.

She and Max had gone upstairs to their room— 'for a quick siesta,' he had told the others, provoking a couple of knowing smiles. And now he lay stretched out on his bed, which stood once more in its original position, side by side with Angela's. He had replaced them this morning to cover their tracks, promising to separate them again tonight.

He leaned back against the pillows, hands clasped behind his head, sighed a deep sigh and closed his eyes. 'You know, I think I might have forty winks, after all. I take it, my dear Angela, that you have no objections?'

Angela had been hovering in the middle of the room, a sudden nervousness assailing her now that they were finally alone. She took a step towards him, arms folded across her chest, and stood awkwardly at the end of his bed.

'I'd rather you didn't, if you don't mind,' she told him. 'I've rather been hoping for a chance to have a chat.'

His eyebrows lifted slightly, but he did not look at her. His eyes remained closed as he observed, 'I see. So that's the reason you've been acting so oddly. I could sense that there was something on your mind.'

Angela pulled a wry face and said nothing for a moment. Had the mantle of self-control she'd been feeling so proud of really been so full of holes?

'Yes,' he continued, still not looking at her. 'You've been decidedly edgy all day. I'm sure no one else noticed, but naturally, as your fiancé, I'm particularly sensitive to your changes of mood.'

So he was in one of those moods when what he enjoyed most was mocking her? Angela began to turn away. 'Perhaps, after all, it would be better if you just slept.' Her enthusiasm for explanations and apologies had somewhat abruptly started to wane.

But halfway across the floor something made her turn round. Perhaps she had felt his eyes on her back. For, as she whirled round to face him, she was surprised to see that he had rolled over on to his side and was lying propped on one elbow, watching her with dark unblinking eyes.

'Come here, my dear Angela.' He patted the bedcover. 'Come here and kindly stop being so sensitive.'

Feeling suddenly confused, Angela hesitated. 'If you'd rather sleep, it really doesn't matter.' Her tone to her dismay sounded piqued and childish. 'What I was going to say to you is really of no importance.'

'Nevertheless, I demand that you come here and say it.' Once again he patted the bedcover. 'And if you don't do as you're told within the count of three, I shall come over there and get you.'

Angela smiled in spite of herself. 'That won't be necessary.' On slow reluctant steps she moved towards him. But she did not seat herself where he had indicated, but rather more distantly on the edge of her own bed.

'So?' He cupped his chin in his hand as he watched her. 'Tell me what it is. I'm all ears.'

Angela folded her hands in her lap and looked down at them. 'I have a confession to make and an apology to offer.' She looked up at him.

He smiled. 'In that order?'

Angela narrowed her eyes at him. She should have been prepared for this, that he would enjoy making a difficult task more difficult.

She sighed a small sigh. 'I'll start with the confession.' She paused, then hurried on, 'It concerns my father.' Then she looked him in the eye and told him without faltering, 'I believed you were responsible for my father's misfortunes. I believed that somehow you'd stolen his money. That was why I came to work for you. To unmask you. And to force you to pay it back.'

She'd been uncertain what reaction she was expecting. Anger, possibly. Justifiable outrage. But she had certainly not been expecting this.

His gaze never flickered. He gave a light shrug. 'I already know that, my dear Angela,' he said.

Angela blinked at him. 'How could you know that? And if you did know, why didn't you say so?'

He smiled. 'I had my reasons for remaining silent.' There was a dark enigmatic look in his eyes. Then he sat up suddenly and swung his legs to the floor, then leaned back once more against the pillows. 'But how I knew is not so hard to figure out. I simply put two and two together. It was perfectly clear that you were searching for something and, since I knew all about your father...' he shrugged '...it was an obvious assumption to make.'

As she frowned at him, feeling oddly deflated—he had seen right through her from the start!—he suddenly straightened and leaned towards her. 'So, how did you figure out that I wasn't the culprit?' He smiled an amused smile. 'I take it that you did?'

'Eventually, yes.' She pulled a self-mocking face. 'The evidence has been staring me in the face all along, but it wasn't until last night that the penny finally dropped.'

She decided to omit that it had come to her in a dream—that would appeal too keenly to his mocking sense of humour. Instead, quite truthfully, she told him, 'I think the realisation began yesterday afternoon when you were discussing possible investments with Sir Gregory...'

'You mean you were eavesdropping?' He feigned disapproval. 'If I'd known, I might have decided to punish you by keeping you in that maze for a little while longer.'

He was smiling, but all the same Angela was quick to assure him, 'I wasn't really trying to eaves-

drop, but he was talking quite loudly. I couldn't
help hearing.'

'You're right, he was, but it was all general stuff
anyway. Nothing particularly personal or private.'
He paused. 'So, what was it you heard, dear
Angela, that decided you that I was innocent?'

Angela smiled fleetingly. Innocent? Max?
Though he undoubtedly was not the villain she had
believed he was, Max and innocence were a contra-
diction in terms!

She paused for a moment to gather her thoughts.
'Well,' she began, 'I heard certain sums men-
tioned. Large sums. Very large. Approaching six
figures...'

As she hesitated, he interjected, 'What's so unusual about that? I deal constantly in sums of that
magnitude. Often much bigger. You know that
from my files.'

Yes, she knew that, but for some reason the sig-
nificance of it hadn't registered until last night.

She took a deep breath. 'My father was one of
your clients. But he was a simple store manager.
He wasn't in that league. By your standards he was
a very minor investor.'

'Minor, perhaps, but important none the less. All
of my clients, whatever the size of their portfolios,
receive the very best advice I can give them.'

Angela nodded. She knew he meant that. 'So,
you see,' she continued, 'why would you risk your
reputation by cheating my poor father out of his
paltry savings, when in a day you can earn more
in the way of commission from the investments of

clients like Sir Gregory? You would have to be crazy. If you wanted to steal, you could steal from the big clients who wouldn't even miss it.'

'Thanks for the advice.' Max was watching her closely, his dark eyes never once straying from her face. 'I'll remember that if I ever decide to go crooked.'

'Oh, I didn't mean that!' Angela was instantly apologetic. 'I was simply illustrating how ridiculous my suspicions were.'

Max smiled. 'Don't worry, I know what you were saying.' Then he reached out suddenly and took hold of her hand. He held it lightly between both of his and he seemed to study her for a moment. 'Besides,' he told her, 'you're the sensitive one. I'm not quite so easily offended.'

Angela tried to ignore the sudden warmth inside her, the strange tingling that extended from the hand he was holding all the way up to the hairs on her scalp, then all the way down again to the tips of her toes.

She could feel her heart beating. She swallowed quickly and prayed that her voice sounded normal as she said to him, 'Still, you must have been just a little bit offended that I—that anyone—could suspect you of such a thing?'

He stroked her hand softly. 'I was intrigued more than offended. I wondered what on earth you were hoping to find. After all——' he smiled softly '—although you're a bright girl, a *very* bright girl, as well as being quite exceptionally lovely, you're not exactly a financial expert. How could you

possibly know what to look for, or how to re-
cognise it, if you found it?'

At his words, a dart of sudden guilt went lancing
through her. She glanced away awkwardly. Should
she tell him the whole story? Should she tell him
that Denis had agreed to help her?

As she looked back at his face she could see quite
clearly that he had caught, and recognised, that
guilty reaction. But though she knew he was waiting
for her to continue, he prompted her neither with
gesture nor word.

This confession is yours, he seemed to be saying.
I know there is more, but I won't force you to tell
me.

Angela took a deep breath. What use was half a
confession? She smiled a quick apologetic smile.
'There was someone who'd promised to give me a
hand to decipher whatever information I could get
hold of.'

'I see.' Still he did not press her. But the expression in his eyes had grown shuttered,
unreadable.

Angela swallowed again. 'It was my cousin,
Denis. He said he would help me interpret the
figures.'

Max nodded slowly. 'Your cousin, Denis?' He
released her hand, so that suddenly she felt cold.
'The same Cousin Denis who is not your lover?'

There was a harshness in his tone that made her
flesh shrink. It seemed so long since she had last
heard that harshness. As he sat back, creating a
chasm between them, she offered apologetically, 'I

know it looks bad. I know it looks as though we were ganging up against you. But you've got to understand... As misguided as it sounds, I did seriously believe that you'd cheated my father.'

'So you said.' He stood up suddenly and looked down at her through narrowed dark eyes. 'And Denis, who is not your lover... did he believe this about me, too?'

'I think so. He said so. It seemed the obvious explanation.' Suddenly, Angela couldn't think straight. Max's sudden change of mood had shocked and confused her. All she could see was his hostility towering over her.

On an impulse she sprang to her feet before him. She reached out to touch his arm apologetically, but withdrew it. 'Look, I'm sorry if what I've been saying has upset you. I know we were wrong now, and I do apologise. I really am deeply, unconditionally sorry.'

An endless moment passed. Max said nothing. His eyes were on her face, intense and searching. Then she started as he reached out to softly touch her cheek. 'Are you, sweet Angela? Are you, really?'

He had spoken the words almost in a whisper, as though addressing the question to himself, not to her. Then he smiled unexpectedly. 'My poor sweet Angela. What a terrible time you've been having. Espionage, I fear, isn't really your game.'

The harshness of before had melted from his voice. Angela shook her head. 'It most definitely isn't.' Then as the tension in her slowly began to dissipate, she looked up into his face. 'I wanted to ask you ... do you have any theories as to what happened to my father's money?'

He held her eyes for a moment. 'I may have,' he answered. He stood very still, continuing to look at her.

'What are they? Please tell me.' She felt a quiver of excitement. 'Please tell me, Max. What theories do you have?'

He continued to look at her. A strange look crossed his face. Then he shook his head. 'Not now, my dear Angela. I think I've had enough of this subject for tonight.' He turned away abruptly. Too abruptly, Angela thought. 'Actually, I need a drink. Can I get you something?'

Angela watched as he crossed to the mini-bar in one corner and proceeded to pour himself a large neat whisky. Why the reluctance? she was wondering. It wasn't like Max to hold back.

Did he know who it was who had cheated her father? As she frowned at his back, a sudden thought occurred to her. Could it be ...? But no. She pushed the thought from her. She was imagining things. And there was probably no mystery. As he had said, he was simply tired of the subject.

As he turned to look at her, she answered his question. 'I'll have a Martini, thanks. Ice and lemon.' She sat down on the bed. He was absolutely right, there'd been enough confessions and explanations for the moment. There'd be plenty of time to return to the subject later.

There was no sign of the strange reticence that had so briefly possessed him as he returned to the bed and handed her her drink. He sat down on his own bed and took a mouthful of his whisky. 'So, how's my fiancée?' His tone was teasing. 'How's she enjoying our little weekend?'

'To her surprise, she's enjoying it immensely. I like your friends. They're very nice people.'

'I knew you'd like them.' He leaned back against the pillows. 'So, do you figure that, perhaps, being my fiancée isn't such a dire fate, after all?'

For some reason, something fluttered strangely inside her. Her fingers tightened a little around her glass. 'Being your *fake* fiancée isn't so terrible. I'm not qualified to pass judgement on being the real thing.'

'No, you aren't, are you?' He regarded her for a moment. Then he smiled and leaned his head back against the pillows. 'I did have a real fiancée once, as I've told you. She seemed to find the experience pretty awful.'

'I don't believe it!' It was out without her thinking. Angela took a gulp of her Martini to cover her embarrassment. Then she added crassly, trying to make a joke of it, 'What on earth did you do to the poor girl?'

Max smiled. 'I don't know, but I sure frightened her off. I was all of nineteen years old at the time. She was twenty-two and I was putty in her hands. But after a couple of months she went off with an old boyfriend and left me nursing a broken heart.'

'You mean the engagement only lasted a couple of months?'

'Two months, one week and three days exactly.'

'And you were broken-hearted?' She squinted across at him. It was difficult to know if he was joking or serious.

'I was for a while.' His expression had sobered. 'But at nineteen, luckily, one's heart mends quickly.' He shook his head. 'Still, it taught me a lesson. Love is not a game, it's a serious business. The human heart is not something to be trifled with.'

He drained his glass and smiled across at her. 'So, what about you, my dear, sweet Angela? Has anyone ever broken your heart?'

'Not seriously, no.'

'Not even that chap you told me about?'

'Andy? No.' Angela shook her head. 'I was disappointed and very sad for a while, but he certainly didn't break my heart.' She shrugged. 'I'm afraid I've never really been in love. I'm still waiting for the big one to come along.' As she said it, foolishly, she glanced away from him. 'If it ever comes,' she added, embarrassed.

'It'll come. Don't worry.' Angela heard him stand up. His hand brushed her hair, making her scalp tingle. 'It'll come, I suspect, when you least expect it. That's the way these things usually happen.'

She looked up then to find him looking down at her with dark and strangely clouded eyes. She wanted to stand up. She longed to embrace him. It was a crazy impulse, but she could not stop it.

But before she could move, he had turned away. 'I'm going to have a shower now and get changed for dinner.' He glanced at his watch. 'It's getting late. We ought to be downstairs in about three-quarters of an hour.'

As he headed for the bathroom, Angela watched him, fighting the confusion of emotions that drove through her. What was getting into her? She was taking leave of her senses. A long, cold shower would do her good, too.

But in the bathroom doorway he suddenly turned to look at her. 'Do me a favour, Angela,' he requested. 'Wear that red dress of yours again tonight.'

Angela wore the red dress, but with slight reservations, aware that the request had overly pleased her. She was treading a dangerous path, she realised, by putting so much foolish store by his compliments. Compliments came easy to a man like Max.

Yet she sensed, as they sat with the others round the dinner table, that there was an extra warmth in his manner this evening, a flicker of something at the back of his eyes that, she was certain, had not been there before.

Hadn't he told her he found her exceptionally lovely? Hadn't he held her hand? Caressed her hair? Her stomach contracted, her breath caught in her throat, and simultaneously she fought to quell these reactions.

It had meant nothing, she told herself. Kind gestures that meant nothing. It was crazy to dwell on them. She was only kidding herself.

And then she would look into his eyes again and see that flickering promise at the back of them, and a foolish excitement would rise up inside her. How could she deny the evidence of her own eyes? Why should she deny her instincts? Surely it was safe to trust what she could feel?

But there were a million arguments that said she shouldn't, and Angela fought back at herself with every single one of them. And rationality was winning. She could feel it. Common sense was taking control.

It was close to midnight when the guests broke up. Max touched her arm. 'You go on up. I want to have a word with Sir Gregory, if you don't mind.' He threw her a wink. 'I don't know how long I'll be, but I promise I'll try not to wake you up.'

That was plain enough. Angela felt her heart plummet, yet common sense was crowing, I told you so! The things she had seen she had simply imagined. And the truth was, it was better this way.

She undressed quickly and went through to the bathroom. A warm bath, she decided. A very quick one. And then to bed and, hopefully, to sleep.

And she didn't linger. She lay among the bubbles for no more than a scant ten minutes. Then she pulled the lever to drain the water, stood up slowly and reached for a towel.

'How beautiful you are.'

She whirled round with a gasp to see Max standing watching her from the bathroom doorway.

He stepped towards her. 'My sweet, lovely Angela. Come.' With a smile, he held out his hand.

And it was then that Angela did something quite extraordinary. Without a blush, without a flicker of hesitation, she stepped out of the bath and into his arms.

CHAPTER ELEVEN

ANGELA gasped as his arms closed around her.

'I was hoping you'd be waiting,' Max murmured against her hair. 'I completed my business with Sir Gregory extra quickly. I was anxious to come to you. I knew you'd be waiting.' He drew back a little. His eyes searched her face. 'You were waiting, weren't you? You knew that I'd come?'

'I hoped.' She smiled. 'I thought you might not.' She felt suddenly awkward. 'Your business with Sir Gregory... I thought it might keep you. You hinted it might.'

'I feared it might.' He shook his head slowly. 'And also I feared that, even if I came, you might not want me, that I had misread the signals.'

'Oh, no.' She smiled. A blush touched her cheek. She looked up into his face. And still he had not kissed her.

He seemed to read her mind. He brushed her lips with his. 'You know, my sweet Angela, that if I kiss you now...' he brushed her lips again '...if I kiss you properly... that will not be the end of it, that will just be the beginning?'

Angela nodded. 'Yes. I know.'

'One kiss, or even a hundred, could never be enough for me.' His eyes burned hotly. 'I need more than kisses.'

'I, too.' She looked at him. His eyes scorched through her. The sight of his passion made her shiver.

'And you have no reservations?' Still he seemed to hesitate. 'Whatever consequences may ensue, you are quite sure you're prepared to accept them?'

She frowned at him a little. What was he saying? 'You mean the possibility that I might get pregnant?'

He brushed back her hair. 'I wasn't meaning that. Against that particular danger we can take precautions.' His hands cupped her shoulders. He held her at arm's length. 'But other dangers exist, my dear, sweet Angela, against which it is not so easy to defend oneself.' He smiled a rueful smile. 'I refer to the human heart, the human heart which is a complex, unpredictable thing.'

She knew what he was telling her. That she must not fall in love with him. That she must accept, before they took a step further, that what would ensue had no deeper meaning. He would make love to her, but that was where it started and ended. Fundamentally, it would change nothing between them.

Deep inside, a part of her was suddenly bleeding. Could she in all honesty accept such a deal? But she was feeling reckless. She pushed her fear from her. This moment was what mattered. Who cared about tomorrow? And this moment was real. Its brightness filled her soul.

'I accept,' she told him, looking back at him steadily.

He smiled. 'Dear, sweet Angela.' And once more he drew her closer. His lips brushed her hair. She felt her scalp tingle. Then he was taking her by the hand, leading her into the bedroom. 'But, first,' he said, 'let me look at you.'

He held her away from him, his hand clasping hers, and let his eyes drift over her naked body. 'You are beautiful,' he told her. He continued to watch her. 'Beautiful. Perfect. Utterly desirable.' As he spoke, his free hand reached out towards her and lightly caressed one uptilted breast.

The dark eyes that surveyed her seemed to pay her silent homage. And though never before had she stood like this, naked and vulnerable, before any man, Angela felt no embarrassment, no shame.

Her breasts rose and fell as he continued to watch her, but in spite of that warning she knew this was right. It was what she had longed for, what she had secretly waited for. Nothing in the world could have made her walk away.

Still watching her, Max slowly loosened his tie. He slipped off his jacket and tossed it aside, then pulled the tie free and tossed it with the jacket.

'Aren't you going to help me?' He smiled invitingly, as his fingers began to undo the buttons of his shirt.

Angela smiled. 'I'd be glad to.' She stepped towards him, feeling the excitement gather way down deep in the pit of her stomach.

As she reached out, he caught her two hands in his, raised them to his lips and softly kissed them. 'Now they may do their work.' With a smile, he released them, guiding them against the cool cotton of his shirt.

And at the touch of the firm hard contours of his chest, warm and vibrant beneath her questing fingers, she felt the desire in her begin to quicken.

One, two, three. The buttons unfastened easily. Four. She paused, as with the hint of a smile he proceeded to pull his shirt from his trousers, allowing her access to the bottom few buttons. Then he was shrugging the shirt impatiently from his shoulders and pressing her palms against his warm naked chest so that she shuddered and caught her breath quickly.

It was only then that, finally, he kissed her.

Angela felt her heart bounce as his lips made contact, gently at first, plucking tiny, teasing kisses. His arm had slid around her, drawing her to him, so that her breasts were pressed against his bare chest, and she fancied she could feel, as urgent as her own, the hectic beating of his heart.

One hand cradled her head, one arm folded around her shoulders. As he sighed, 'Sweet Angela,' he was drawing her even closer. And her own breath caught as his kiss grew fiercer, his lips devouring her, making her blood leap, igniting passions deep inside her that were new and strange and erotic and wonderful. Then he bent and lifted her into his arms and was carrying her to the nearby bed.

As he laid her on it, he was leaning over her, kissing her mouth, her face, her hair, kissing her throat, her ears, her shoulders, while with one hand he pulled away the rest of his clothing to lie alongside her, naked and hungry.

He held her a moment, his face buried in her hair, his hands unhurriedly caressing her flanks, the dip of her waist, the smoothness of her thighs. And where his hands touched he left a trail of burning flesh, causing Angela to shiver and press against him longingly. And all the while her own hungry hands were smoothing, caressing and exploring, greedily savouring the hard, cool feel of him.

The strong, powerful shoulders, the smoothly muscled back, the hair-roughened chest, the thighs as hard as iron. All of him, every warm-blooded inch of him, she longed to feel beneath her fingers.

'Tell me what you want.' His lips brushed her neck. He kissed her chin, her nose, her ears, before once more hungrily claiming her mouth. Then when she did not answer—for foolish shame had sealed her lips—and simply clung to him, returning his kisses with a passion, he smiled a soft smile. 'In that case,' he murmured, 'I shall have to discover for myself.'

He moved against her. 'How about this?' His hand caressed her, sweeping in one movement from shoulder to thigh, then tantalisingly slowly retracing its path upwards till at last it closed around her burning breast.

His hand moved against her slowly, circling, moulding, moving from one breast to the other. And like a band of steel, the desire in her was tightening, making her breath catch roughly in her throat.

Then she shuddered as he whispered, 'How about this? Is this to your liking, my sweet Angela?' His fingers, as he said it, lightly grazed one hard nipple and she could not quench the moan that rose from her throat as a dart of sheer intense, exquisite pleasure went tearing like a knife through her loins.

'Ah, yes . . .' He was peppering little kisses across her breastbone, as his fingers continued to tease the throbbing peaks, igniting her flesh with slow-burning pleasure.

Then he was shifting against her so that she could feel his own hunger pressing against her, as hard as a bone. A shiver went through her. Raw longing clutched her throat. 'Max!' she murmured. Her lips searched for his mouth. She pressed against him, quivering with desire.

He was sliding on top of her, kneeling between her thighs, pausing for a moment to look into her eyes, as he cupped her two aching breasts in his hands. Then he bent his head and her stomach contracted as a moment later he drew between his lips the hard, taut, eager blood-gorged nipple.

He drew her flesh into his mouth almost fiercely, his teeth grazing her softly, his tongue strumming a cruel torment, and all at once her flesh turned to liquid. The hunger in her was beating like a drum.

Her fingers reached for his hair, tightening in its thickness. The pleasure was so exquisite that she could scarcely bear it.

I want you! her mind thundered. I want you now! And the words were ringing so loudly in her head that it seemed impossible he could not hear them.

If he could, he did not obey them. He had not finished with her yet. As his lips continued their slow, sublime torment, his hand continued with unhurried thoroughness to caress and arouse all her secret places.

Max, please! As her back arched helplessly against him, she could feel the helpless trembling of her thighs. She could scarcely breathe now. Every inch of her burned.

Max! Please! Now! But he paused a moment more to kiss each hungry breast in turn, then to scatter more kisses over her stomach and thighs, before at last leaning over her, pushing the hair from her face and bending to kiss her once more on the lips while lowering his muscular body down on hers.

His voice thick with emotion, he told her, 'I cannot wait. My darling, I must have you now.'

In response, Angela sighed and drew him closer. Then in one movement his manhood slipped between her thighs.

'Now you are mine.' He thrust deeper. 'Completely.'

After, they lay and spoke until dawn—about their lives, their friends, their families, their work.

'Tell me everything about yourself,' Max had demanded, kissing her. 'I want to know every single detail.'

And so she had. She'd told him about growing up in Cambridge, the happy days she'd spent with Jill at college doing secretarial and business studies,

and all the hard work of the past three years getting
Ace Personnel off the ground.

'I'm impressed,' he'd told her. 'You're really
quite a girl.'

And, in return, he had told her all about his own
life—about his parents and his childhood in
London, about his career as a banker before he went
solo.

When finally, exhausted, they drifted off to sleep,
arms wrapped tightly around one another, Angela
felt that a bond had been forged between them. She
was faintly astonished at how deeply happy that
made her feel.

It was only as they were preparing to leave next
morning that it struck her that there was one thing
that Max still hadn't told her—his theory about
what had happened to her father's money.

I shall bring up the subject on the journey home,
she decided, feeling a sharp charge of optimism at
the prospect. Knowing Max, his theory was almost
certainly right.

It was just before nine when they left Lane Park
for the homeward journey back to Cambridge.
Their host and hostess stood in the driveway and
waved them off as they drove away.

'Did you enjoy yourself?' Max glanced across at
her.

Angela smiled. 'Enormously. I love this place.
And Janie and Alan are super hosts.'

'In that case, I may invite you again.'

He said it lightly. Perhaps he was joking. As hope
and fear mingled inside her, Angela suddenly

realised how vulnerable she was feeling. Where did they go from here? Would there be a future? She had felt a bond between them, but had he felt it, too?

Fear gripped her heart like icy fingers. In the space of a few hours something drastic had happened to her. She could no longer bear the thought of a future without Max.

As they headed for the main road, she turned away and tried to focus her thoughts on the present. Perhaps now was the time to bring up the subject of her father.

She turned to look at him. 'You know,' she reminded him, 'you still haven't told me your theory about my father. Tell me now,' she invited. 'I'm dying to hear it. I want to see how plausible it sounds.'

He did not answer her immediately, and as his brows drew together, she could sense his reluctance. Why? she wondered. For what possible reason? Then he shot her a quick glance. 'Oh, it's perfectly plausible. Its plausibility is not the problem.'

Angela regarded him curiously. 'Then what is the problem?'

Max sighed. 'The problem is that I fear you may not like it. That's the reason I've been in no particular hurry to tell you.'

'Not like it? Why?' She felt suddenly nervous. What on earth was he going to say?

Max took a deep breath. 'Before I begin, I must emphasise that part of this is just my personal theory. I have very little proof. Nothing conclusive. But in my own mind I'm a hundred and one per cent certain—and I intend to get the proof that will prove I'm right.'

The nervousness inside her was beginning to tighten. He made what was coming sound rather sinister. 'I wish you'd just go ahead and tell me,' Angela insisted. 'Then I can decide for myself whether I like it or not.'

'OK.' He kept his eyes fixed on the road ahead of them. 'You asked for it and here it is. Your father was being blackmailed.'

'*Blackmailed*? *My father*?' Angela swung round in her seat, indignation flashing from her eyes. 'What do you mean by making such an insulting suggestion? My father was a good and honest man. How could anyone possibly blackmail him?'

Max sighed. 'I told you you wouldn't like it. But I'm afraid it happens to be true.'

'No, it's not! It's only your theory. And if you ask me, your theory stinks!'

'I'm sorry, Angela, but that part isn't theory. I haven't come to the theory part yet. I know for a fact that your father was being blackmailed and the reason I know is because he told me.'

As her face paled, he shook his head apologetically. 'I knew this wasn't going to be easy.' Then on an impulse he took a sudden sharp turning off the main highway and drew up a few yards down a narrow side-road.

He pulled on the hand-brake and turned to look at her. 'Listen to me, Angela. I'm as sorry as you

are. I knew your father and respected him greatly.
But the fact is that he had some secret in his past
that someone found out about and decided to exploit. It could happen to almost any of us. We all
have little secrets that in ruthless hands could be
used to damage us.'

She knew he was trying to soften the impact of
the bomb that had just blown up in her face. But
all the same she hated him for what he had told
her. How could this man who last night had made
love to her wound her now with such tales about
her father?

She pulled her hands free. 'Why did he tell *you*?
Why didn't he tell his wife, his family? Why on
earth did he tell a complete stranger?'

'I wasn't a complete stranger. We'd known each
other for a while. But the reason he came to me
was for practical help. He thought I could help him
recoup some of the money that had been stolen
from him by the blackmailer. He was worried, you
see, about you and your mother. He knew he had
a bad heart. He knew he might die. He was terrified of leaving you with nothing.'

Angela stared into her lap. She swallowed hard.
She felt like weeping. She could not answer him.

'What he asked me to do was invest his remaining money—in something high risk, he was
adamant about that, in something that could make
him a lot of money quickly. Or lose it all quickly.
I warned him of that.'

Angela turned to look at him. 'And you lost it?'

'I didn't lose it. Quite the opposite. Within a very short period he made a substantial gain. But it was a waste of effort. The blackmailer was greedy. Soon these new profits he had made were gone, too.'

'And then? Did he invest more?' Angela looked at him miserably. She believed him now. Every word he was telling her. And his revelation filled her with anger and bitter bile.

As Max looked back at her in silence for a moment, his expression guarded, she urged him to continue. 'What happened next? Did he keep on investing? Did he keep on giving his profits to the blackmailer?' As she threw the words at him she was suddenly filled with an overwhelming sense of resentment. In an angry flood she let her feelings out. 'Go on, don't spare me any details! No doubt you're enjoying telling me all this!'

Max ignored that final hysterical little outburst. 'Yes,' he said, 'he continued to invest and he continued to pay his profits to the blackmailer.'

He glanced out of the window and took a deep breath. 'I kept urging him to go to the police, to put an end to it all before he was ruined. But he refused point-blank. He wouldn't even speak of it. He knew that what he was hiding would all come out then and that your mother would find out.' He turned round to look at her. 'That was what he was most afraid of—your mother discovering what the blackmail was about.'

Angela's hands were twisted tightly in her lap. 'And did he tell you what the blackmail was about?'

'No, he didn't, and I didn't ask. I figured that was really none of my business.' There was a momentary silence, then Max leaned once more towards her and laid one hand softly over both of hers. 'However, I did make it my business to try to uncover the blackmailer—with the intention of dealing with him myself. But before I'd succeeded, sadly, your father died.'

There was a brief, bitter silence as each for a moment contained the memory of that sad loss. Then Max spoke again. 'But although it's too late to help your father, I now know who the blackmailer was.' He looked straight at her. 'The blackmailer was Denis.'

'*Denis*?'

Something turned sickly inside her. Somehow she had known he was going to accuse Denis. That was the suspicion that had crossed her mind last night when Max had been so reluctant to talk about his theory. It was a suspicion, she realised now, he had planted in her head when he had first accused Denis of being her accomplice.

But every fibre of her being rejected his accusation. She looked back at him now with outrage in her eyes. 'That's utterly ridiculous! Denis is my cousin! Denis wouldn't blackmail my father!'

Max's dark brows drew together. 'I appreciate your outrage. The scenario of the young man who steals from the uncle who took him in and gave him a home when he was orphaned is one that I find extremely distasteful. But I'm afraid that's what happened.' As she was about to protest, he cut in quickly with a question. 'Did Denis ever quarrel with your father? As far as you know, did they ever fall out?'

'Of course they didn't! Over the years they lost touch, but I've never heard tell of any quarrel.'

Max shook his head. 'I think there was one. There must have been, to explain such treachery.'

'But there was no treachery!' Angela was adamant. Max might think he knew everything, but he didn't! 'Look at the facts! Denis has no money! His house is rented! He doesn't even own a decent car! Does that sound like the lifestyle of a man who has stolen tens of thousands of pounds?'

Max narrowed his eyes at her. 'Try this for size... A six-bedroom house, complete with Jacuzzi and heated swimming pool, and a brand-new BMW in the garage.' As Angela's mouth dropped open, he added in an even tone, 'But not in Cambridge, I'll grant you that. He's wily enough to keep his spoils hidden—in Wiltshire, which is where he lives when he's not in Cambridge.'

The story was becoming more and more preposterous. Angela threw him a cool look. 'Do you expect me to believe all this? I've never heard anything so crazy in my life.'

'Not crazy, clever. No one suspects him. His old buddies in Cambridge see him living just the same, dressed in his shabby suits with never a penny to his name, and his new friends in Wiltshire have no reason to suspect that the comfortable life he leads there has not been earned.'

'Are you trying to tell me he's leading a double life? I don't believe you. You're making it all up.'

Max shot her a glance. 'So check out my story.' He quickly reeled off an address in Wiltshire. 'Go and see for yourself if I'm lying.'

'I wouldn't waste my time.' Angela turned away angrily, then swivelled round sharply to dissect him with a look. 'What I'm wondering is why you're making up this story. A few minutes ago I was almost believing you, but what you're telling me now is beyond belief.' She narrowed her eyes at him. 'What are you hiding? Is this whole stupid story some kind of cover?'

She wished she had not said it, for she did not believe it and she knew it had sounded nasty and vindictive. But he had tied her brain in knots with his unspeakable theory. How could Denis, whom she had known since she was twelve, do such a terrible thing to her father?

Max did not answer her, he simply looked at her with eyes that had grown as hard as granite, silencing the apology that hovered on her lips. Then he switched on the engine, did a quick U-turn and headed back towards the highway.

'Oh, by the way,' he said at last in a tone as harsh as his expression, 'as soon as we get back I shall be releasing you from my employ. And that,' he added, catching her eye, 'will be the end, in all senses, of our uncomfortable liaison. You and I, dear Angela, as anyone can see, really have no more to offer one another.'

'I couldn't agree more.' It was a reflex action, an effort to fight off for one defiant moment longer the coldness that was closing like a dead hand round her heart. She tore the fake engagement ring from her finger and thrust it at him as she added vindictively, 'But then you and I never really did have anything worthwhile to offer one another.'

'No,' he agreed. 'I'm well aware of that.' He pocketed the ring without even a glance at her and pressed his foot down hard on the accelerator, as though he suddenly could not wait for the journey to be over and for them to go their separate ways.

CHAPTER TWELVE

THAT was it. Over so swiftly. Ended almost before it had decently begun.

Back at Denis's apartment, Angela sat in an armchair, her still unpacked case dropped in a corner. She stared unseeingly at the fireplace. I could have loved Max. I came so close to it. I was within an inch of giving him my heart.

She closed her eyes and clenched her fists tightly. How come, if she had only come close to loving him, was she now feeling so utterly wretched? How come, if there had still been an inch to go, did she feel as though her heart had been crushed to powder?

She drew her knees up against her chest and wrapped her arms round them, making herself small. Why did she feel as though her life had been severed? As though her will, her strength had all been drained from her, as though her soul had been pillaged and left a wilderness? Why did she feel she would never smile again?

She pressed her face against her knees to staunch the flow of tears that threatened. But the harder she pressed, the more freely they flowed. Like the pain in her heart, there was no end to them.

* * *

'Angela, sit down. I want to talk to you. Perhaps
I know more than your father ever realised.'

From the green velvet sofa by the window Mrs
Smith smiled sadly across at her daughter, who was
pacing restlessly about the sitting-room. 'This secret
of your father's that he was being blackmailed over.
I know what it was. I've always known about it.
Though I didn't know, of course, that he was being
blackmailed.' A tear rolled down her cheek. 'If only
I had.'

Angela had seated herself in one of the arm-
chairs and was watching her mother through narrowed misty eyes. What was she about to hear now?
she wondered. Over the past couple of days there
had been so many revelations, so many discoveries
that had sent her reeling. Can I cope, she wondered, with yet another one?

She had gone straight to Wiltshire the day after
her return, to the address that Max had quoted,
and watched, hidden, outside. And she had seen
Denis and she had seen the big BMW and she had
known that what Max had told her was true.

Her instinctive reaction had been to confront her
cousin, to knock on his door and beat him with
her fists. But wisdom had prevailed. Why reveal
her hand and provide him with a chance to escape?
No, she must bide her time, as Max was doing, until
she was sure of her case against him. And, in the
meantime, she must speak to her mother.

Mrs Smith had been shocked when Angela had
shared with her her own and Max's suspicions about

Denis—but not nearly as surprised as Angela had expected.

She had remained silent for a moment. 'Yes, that fits,' she'd murmured. 'So, finally, he carried out his threat.'

Angela had frowned across at her. 'What threat are you talking about?'

Her mother sat back in the sofa. 'It was a long time ago. You were still very young. I doubt you ever suspected what was going on. But less than a year after he moved in here, Denis quarrelled with your father. It wasn't the first quarrel, but it was the most violent. He was a difficult young man, always demanding money, and when your father refused to increase his allowance they had the most terrible, violent row.'

She had paused, remembering. 'I didn't take it seriously. People say things they don't mean when they're angry. But he promised your father that one day he would ruin him.' A sob caught in her throat. 'Quite clearly, he meant it.'

Angela had listened, scarcely believing. So, Max had been right. There had been a quarrel. Inwardly, she had sighed. How blind she had been. There were so many things she had never suspected.

And now her mother was about to tell her about her father's secret. She held her breath and waited, literally prepared for anything.

As it transpired, it was a predictable enough story. Her father had had a mistress many years ago, while she herself was just a baby. Her mother had found out long after the affair was over.

Mrs Smith shrugged sadly. 'I said nothing to your father. To have stirred it all up would only have done damage and my marriage was the most precious thing in the world to me.'

Angela rose from her seat and crossed to the sofa. She sat down beside her mother and put an arm around her. 'I think it must have been pretty precious to my father, too, that he was prepared to ruin himself to keep his secret from you. He really must have loved you very deeply.'

Angela drove back to Denis's apartment next morning, her mother's last words ringing in her ears. 'Go to that friend of yours. Tell him what I've told you. Then contact the police and have Denis arrested: I don't care if the story all comes out. Denis must pay for what he did to your father.'

Go to that friend of yours. Angela's heart skittered forlornly. Max was no friend of hers, and how could she go to him? She could scarcely even bear to think of him. Each time she did, she died a little.

But she had to do it. She had promised her mother. And, in a way, it was only right that she should. Max had been working for a long time to trap Denis. It would be wrong of her not to share with him this new information. He deserved to be in at the kill.

She summoned all her courage once she was back at the office to dial his number and let it ring. The thought of speaking to him, of hearing his voice again, literally terrified her. She was bound to fall apart again.

But it was his reinstalled secretary who answered. 'I'm sorry, he's not here, and I have no other number. If you'd like to leave a message, I'll pass it on next time he calls.'

Angela left a message, though it was a gesture more than anything. The last thing he was likely to do was call her. A pain lanced through her. In all probability, the reason he'd left town was to get away from her.

So, what should she do now? Should she go to the police without him? She frowned into space, undecided. He had proof, he had told her, and, though it was not conclusive, the police, no doubt, would wish to hear it.

With a sigh she glanced at the calendar on her desk. Denis was due back at the end of the week, so it was absolutely essential that she act before then. She would give Max until Thursday to contact her, and then, if she still hadn't heard from him, she would act alone.

Again the pain went sweeping through her, even fiercer than before. She knew she was fooling herself by waiting. Max would not contact her, ever again.

On Wednesday night Angela worked late at the office, making up for the burden she had placed on Jill during her absence by clearing up an almost ceiling-high stack of paperwork that was outstanding.

It was after ten when she glanced at her watch and decided it was time she went back to the flat.

Though she was reluctant to leave. Working here in the office, she could almost succeed in driving Max from her mind, a feat she was incapable of when she was at home.

Besides, these past days she'd hated staying at the flat, knowing what she now knew about her cousin. Every stick of furniture turned her stomach. She could scarcely wait to be gone.

But tonight, thank heavens, would be her very last night there. Tomorrow she'd be moving in with Jill and Eddie, just until she found a place of her own. She sat back in her seat and stared at the newspaper, whose small ads she had studied earlier, looking for a place to rent. Tomorrow she had a clutch of appointments with estate agents and she had already decided to take the first place she was offered.

She sighed tiredly and flicked idly at the pages of the newspaper. But first, tomorrow morning, she had an appointment with the police. As she'd expected, there'd been no word from Max, so it was up to her to expose Denis herself. Once he returned, should he wish to re-involve himself, Max could go to the police station independently and make whatever contribution to the case he felt like making.

But suddenly her thoughts were interrupted as her eye alighted on a two-column article tucked away at the foot of the business pages. She leaned closer to examine it, her heart beating strangely. It was a report on the case of dishonest dealing that had been brought against that ex-colleague of Max's.

As she read it, she was aware of a sense of satisfaction to learn not only that Max's friend had been acquitted, but that he had also been offered an apology by the court that the case should ever have been brought against him. It appeared that the evidence against him had been rigged.

Angela sat back in her seat and closed her eyes wearily. Denis had used this case, and Max's links with the defendant, to help convince her of his immorality. And she, naïvely, had fallen for the tactic. How easily she had let herself be led.

She stood up now and gathered together her things. There was so much she knew now that she hadn't known then. So much that had happened. So much that had changed.

She snapped her bag shut. Herself, for example. She was no longer the person she had been a few weeks ago. In those far-off days, as distant as another lifetime, her heart had been her own, she had been full of confidence, not dreading, as she did now, every step into the future. The lonely, worthless future without Max that stretched ahead of her like a desert.

She moved away from the desk, impatient with herself, wishing she could heal the anguish in her heart. You knew, she chided. You knew it would happen. That night when he caught you in the bathroom, he warned you. And you knew anyway. But you were foolish, you were reckless. You dared to hope. And now you must pay the price.

She drove slowly, reluctantly, back to the flat, but as she rounded the final corner her heart stopped within her—for there, parked right in front of the apartment block, like a threatening dark shadow, stood a black Rolls-Royce.

Angela very nearly turned around and fled. Instantly, her hand was hovering over the gear stick. But already the door of the Rolls had opened and the tall figure of Max was climbing out.

Her breath caught jaggedly. It was almost like a miracle to see him striding so purposefully towards her. This man whom she loved and who would never be hers. This man whom she had feared she might never see again.

Stiff with misery, she pulled into the kerb, just as he came abreast of the driver's door. Then, as she slipped on the hand-brake, he was pulling the door open.

'Where have you been? I've been waiting!' he snapped.

'Waiting?' She looked at him. Her brain was barely functioning. All she knew was the pain that jarred within her at the sight of his adored and angry face.

'Where have you been?' He was stepping aside as she climbed out awkwardly on to the road beside him.

She tore her gaze away from him. 'I've been at the office. I've been working late. I had work to catch up on.'

'Till this hour?' He scowled at her and glanced at his watch. 'Do you normally work until after ten-thirty?'

His attitude angered her. She resented his aggression. She looked him in the eye. 'When I choose to I do,' she answered. 'Do you have any particular objection?'

'As a matter of fact, I have.' His tone had not softened. 'I've been waiting here since half-past seven.'

He had taken her arm. Angela snatched herself free of him. 'Don't blame me. I didn't know you were here. And, anyway, it's I who should be angry. I left a message with your secretary hours ago and you haven't even bothered to ring me.'

'I didn't get the message until this afternoon. And I didn't bother to call because I'd decided to come in person. Why?' He looked down at her, his dark eyes narrowing. 'Did you have any particular reason for wishing to speak to me?'

As he said it, it struck Angela that perhaps he was thinking that her request had had a personal motive. Perhaps he believed that she had been intending to beg for a repeat of Sunday night.

She dared not look at him lest she see that in his face. To see such a cheap assumption would be crushing. She took a shaky step towards the pavement and informed him with only a brief glance across her shoulder, 'I wanted to speak to you about Denis. I've been to see my mother and I know now you were right about him. He did quarrel with my father, and he blackmailed him, I'm certain. Tomorrow I plan to report him to the police.'

Max was looking down at her, black eyebrows drawn together. 'I see,' he murmured. Then he took her by the arm again. 'I suggest we go indoors to continue this discussion. It would be rather more comfortable than standing in the street.'

Angela pulled away from him. 'There's nothing to discuss. You were right and I've acknowledged that.' She cleared her throat. 'If you like, you can come with me to the police tomorrow. Then you can tell them what you know.'

In spite of her withdrawal, Max had not released her arm. His grip had simply tightened slightly. 'I shall do that too.' He propelled her across the pavement. 'But first, we're going upstairs to the flat.'

There was as much point in arguing with him as in arguing with a bulldozer. It was perfectly clear he intended to have his way.

Angela ceased to resist and looked coldly up at him. 'OK, if you insist, that's the way we'll do it.' She jerked her arm free. 'But, if you don't mind, I'm capable of walking without assistance from you.'

As he released her with a wry smile, she stepped ahead of him swiftly and strode through the front door to the lift. His nearness seemed to choke her. She could neither breathe nor think straight. She took a deep breath and tried desperately to calm herself. She must not shame herself by revealing her emotions. She must force herself to behave calmly and rationally.

She gritted her teeth. Somehow she would do it.

Once in the flat he went through to the sitting-room and sat down on the sofa without an invitation. He unbuttoned his jacket, leaned back and looked at her. 'I've spent the last two days in the City,' he told her, 'picking the brains of some banking friends of mine. And now, thanks to their influence and their know-how, I have gathered all the proof against Denis that I need. As I suspected, every penny of your father's money was paid over the years into his various accounts.

'I have all the figures, dates and details that the prosecution will need to throw your cousin into gaol.'

As she listened, for a moment Angela forgot her own anguish. The weight that had oppressed her since her father's death, at last, miraculously, had lifted.

He said what she was thinking. 'Your father will be avenged and the money Denis stole—at least the part he hasn't spent—will naturally be returned to your mother.' Then he smiled. 'And there's one unexpected bright spot. The money he hasn't spent, he invested—and, I'll say this for him, he invested cleverly. The profits from these investments more or less make up for what he has already spent.'

Angela's brows rose. 'That's absolutely wonderful.' Then she smiled at him in genuine gratitude. 'Thank you,' she told him, 'for all you've done. You didn't need to do it. I appreciate it greatly.'

Max shrugged. 'Don't thank me. I couldn't have done otherwise. I respected your father. I was even rather fond of him. I was as anxious as you were to track down the man who had ruined him.'

She could see he meant it. Her heart swelled within her. No wonder she loved him. He was a good and caring man.

Tears sprang to her eyes. She lowered her gaze sharply and tried to fight them back, staring at her hands.

'What about you?' She could feel his gaze on her. 'You said you'd been to see your mother... What exactly did she tell you?'

In a small voice she told him, omitting no details. 'I can still scarcely believe,' she ended sadly, 'that Denis could do such a thing to my father.'

There was a momentary silence. 'Not only to your father. Cousin Denis had other victims as well.'

Angela glanced up then. 'Are you serious? Are you telling me he was some kind of professional blackmailer?'

'He was heading that way. He started with your father, then when that worked so well he found other victims.' His eyes narrowed as he looked at her. 'It was something I'd suspected and that was why...' He broke off and frowned, looking deep into her eyes. 'That was why I believed he was out to blackmail me.'

Angela's eyes flew wide open. 'Blackmail you? What could he possibly blackmail you about?'

'Nothing that I'm aware of.' Max smiled wryly. 'But at the time there was that court case going on with me tenuously linked to the defendant. To someone with a mind like Denis's, you must admit, it was worth a try.'

Angela nodded. From a victim like Max a black-mailer might hope for rich pickings indeed. Except for the fact, she found herself amending, that a man like Max would be a bad choice for blackmail. Whatever else he was, he was nobody's victim.

He leaned towards her. 'I have a confession. About you and Denis.' He paused for an instant.

Angela frowned at him. 'What sort of con-fession?' All at once there was a strange look in his eyes.

Max sighed. 'It concerns my decision to OK my secretary's request that we use your agency instead of our usual one—the decision that led to your coming to work for me.'

He leaned forward a fraction, his eyes boring into her. 'At the time, as I've told you, I was under the impression that you and Denis were working together. I had a suspicion that the arrangement with my secretary was a ruse to allow you to come and work for me—so that you could spy on me on Denis's behalf and try and uncover some basis for blackmail. I decided to go along with it for the very simple reason that I thought it would give me a chance to spy on you and Denis.'

He shook his head wryly. 'So you see, my dear Angela, while you were spying on me, I was spying on you. A most unsavoury situation.'

Angela blinked across at him. 'You mean,' she said, astounded, 'that you truly believed that I might have been involved in the blackmailing of my own father?'

'It didn't take me long to realise I was wrong, to become convinced that you weren't Denis's accomplice at all, that in fact you'd come to work for me for a very different reason—because you believed I'd ruined your father.' He sighed. 'But the answer to your question is yes. In the beginning I did believe that.'

He leaned towards her and smiled at her gently. 'Don't look so horrified. After all, what you believed of me was pretty nasty too.'

But Angela didn't smile back. 'How could you?' she blurted out. 'How could you think such a despicable thing?'

'I'm sorry,' he told her and reached out towards her to take one of her hands firmly in his. 'I'm sorry about a lot of things. I'd no idea that things would turn out as they did.'

Angela tried to snatch her hand away. She felt mortally wounded. 'You should have known!' she accused him. 'If you were any judge of character, you would have known right away that I couldn't be Denis's accomplice!'

Max shook his head. 'That's not what I meant.' He looked into her eyes, holding her hand firmly. 'When I said I didn't know how things would turn out, I wasn't referring to you and Denis.'

'Then what were you referring to?' Now he was confusing her. And the way he was holding her hand so tightly and looking at her with that strange look

in his eyes was making her stomach clench inside
her. She had never seen that look before.

'I meant . . .' Still holding her hand, he stood up,
forcing her to stand up with him. 'Perhaps I
shouldn't say this.' He looked into her eyes. 'For
in your heart of hearts I'm not at all sure that you
have totally changed your opinion of me.

'But what the hell? I'm going to say it anyway,'
he continued before she could interrupt him. 'What
I meant, my dear Angela, was that I had no idea
that I was going to fall in love with you.'

His words were like a firecracker going off in her
face. Confused, bright colours flashed before her
eyes, blinding her, rendering her silent. Surely, she
was telling herself, she must have misheard him.
He could not have told her that he loved her.

But as she gaped at him, speechless, he said it
again. 'I love you, Angela. Pure and simple. I think
I started to fall in love with you soon after I met
you, but it wasn't until that night at Lane Park that
I realised I was on the brink of something I could
no longer control.'

He smiled. 'I warned you before we made love
that I was in danger of falling in love with you.'
He reached out to stroke her hair. 'I asked you if
you were prepared to accept the consequences that
might ensue from our making love—namely the fact
that once I had fallen in love with you I would continue to pursue you until the day I died.'

Angela's cheeks had grown as pale as parchment.
As she stared at him in silence, he drew her to him.
'Is that all you have to say?' he teased her, kissing

her. But behind the light words she could sense that he was aching.

She tilted her head up to look into his face. 'I misunderstood.' Her voice was husky. 'I thought you were warning me that it would be dangerous for me to fall in love with you.'

His eyes widened in surprise. 'I would not have presumed.' He broke off abruptly and gazed at her intently. 'Would such a warning have been appropriate? Was there any danger of such a thing?'

'Oh, Max!' She kissed him, her heart grown huge within her. 'There was every danger! I was falling in love with you, too!'

'But——'

She covered his lips with one finger to stop his protest. 'I know what I said to you that time in the car. I know it sounded as though I still didn't trust you. But I was shocked and upset. I didn't know what I was saying.' She let her fingers slide round to the back of his head. 'I think I was in love with you even before we made love.'

Max pulled her to him and held her tightly for a moment. 'Oh, Angela,' he murmured against her hair, 'what a pair of fools we've been.' His lips sought hers. 'I love you, my darling. Say you'll marry me. That's all I wish.'

They were married less than two months later, and it was as grand a wedding as the city of Cambridge had ever seen.

Mrs Smith wept copiously as she watched her beautiful daughter being led down the aisle on the arm of her uncle to join the handsome, proudly smiling groom at the altar. And even Jill had a sob or two into her hankie.

'Are you happy, my darling?' Max murmured softly, as, vows pledged and rings exchanged, they walked arm in arm, husband and wife at last, back down the aisle.

'Oh, yes,' she nodded. She glanced at him. 'And you?'

'Happier than I could ever express.' He smiled and bent to kiss her briefly, causing her heart, so full of joy already, to overflow with perfect happiness.

Then, arms still entwined, clasping her hand tightly, he led her out through the open church door into a bright winter's day, filled with sunshine.

And in the years to come it would always seem to Angela that it was at that precise moment that her life really began.

HARLEQUIN®

Don't miss these Harlequin favorites by some of our most distin-
guished authors!
And now, you can receive a discount by ordering two or more titles!

HT#25409	THE NIGHT IN SHINING ARMOR by JoAnn Ross	$2.99	☐
HT#25471	LOVESTORM by JoAnn Ross	$2.99	☐
HP#11463	THE WEDDING by Emma Darcy	$2.89	☐
HP#11592	THE LAST GRAND PASSION by Emma Darcy	$2.99	☐
HR#03188	DOUBLY DELICIOUS by Emma Goldrick	$2.89	☐
HR#03248	SAFE IN MY HEART by Leigh Michaels	$2.89	☐
HS#70464	CHILDREN OF THE HEART by Sally Garrett	$3.25	☐
HS#70524	STRING OF MIRACLES by Sally Garrett	$3.39	☐
HS#70500	THE SILENCE OF MIDNIGHT by Karen Young	$3.39	☐
HI#22178	SCHOOL FOR SPIES by Vickie York	$2.79	☐
HI#22212	DANGEROUS VINTAGE by Laura Pender	$2.89	☐
HI#22219	TORCH JOB by Patricia Rosemoor	$2.89	☐
HAR#16459	MACKENZIE'S BABY by Anne McAllister	$3.39	☐
HAR#16466	A COWBOY FOR CHRISTMAS by Anne McAllister	$3.39	☐
HAR#16462	THE PIRATE AND HIS LADY by Margaret St. George	$3.39	☐
HAR#16477	THE LAST REAL MAN by Rebecca Flanders	$3.39	☐
HH#28704	A CORNER OF HEAVEN by Theresa Michaels	$3.99	☐
HH#28707	LIGHT ON THE MOUNTAIN by Maura Seger	$3.99	☐

Harlequin Promotional Titles

#83247	YESTERDAY COMES TOMORROW by Rebecca Flanders	$4.99	☐
#83257	MY VALENTINE 1993	$4.99	☐
	(short-story collection featuring Anne Stuart, Judith Arnold, Anne McAllister, Linda Randall Wisdom)		

(limited quantities available on certain titles)

	AMOUNT	$	
DEDUCT:	10% DISCOUNT FOR 2+ BOOKS	$	
ADD:	POSTAGE & HANDLING	$	
	($1.00 for one book, 50¢ for each additional)		
	APPLICABLE TAXES*	$ _____	
	TOTAL PAYABLE	$ _____	
	(check or money order—please do not send cash)		

To order, complete this form and send it, along with a check or money order for the
total above, payable to Harlequin Books, to: **In the U.S.:** 3010 Walden Avenue,
P.O. Box 9047, Buffalo, NY 14269-9047; **In Canada:** P.O. Box 613, Fort Erie, Ontario,
L2A 5X3.

Name: _____

Address: _____ City: _____

State/Prov.: _____ Zip/Postal Code: _____

*New York residents remit applicable sales taxes.
Canadian residents remit applicable GST and provincial taxes.

HBACK-JM